CACTUS
GIRLS

ALSO BY SANDY DAL SANTO

Fiction

Don't Whisper in My Ear

Cactus Girls

CACTUS GIRLS

Sandy Dal Santo

Lake House Publishing
Fountain Hills, Arizona
sdalsanto.lakehousepublishing@gmail.com

TABLE OF CONTENTS

My mother was my life long sorrow

It seemed like yesterday
When I was so young
I found myself alone
In the darkness
I never needed anyone

I'm getting back on the road now
I know a thing or two

I'm ready to forget everything I've learned from you

I am ready to be me.

ONE

Breckenridge, June 1980

No Chains Around My Feet, But I Am Not Free

"Children are to be seen and not heard," mother would whisper in my ear when I was younger. But, not anymore. I belonged to nobody. Her famous words still echoed over and over while I shoved clothes into my backpack and zipped it up. There was a shuffling noise at my bedroom door. I looked up to find Kelsey, Karen and Dan's four-year-old daughter standing in the doorway.

"Where are you going, Sandy?"

"My friend Holly and I are going on a little trip."

"Who's Holly?" Kelsey asked.

"Holly is my best friend from Chicago, where I lived before I moved to Breckenridge last September."

Holly and I were driving out West, where I'd been told the fallen sun met the ocean at the end of each day and new days always started tomorrow. A new day, a new life, a new me.

"When will you be back?"

"I'm not sure, but I'll be back before your birthday in September." Kelsey's eyes lit up. "And how old are you going to be when I return?"

She raised her hand and spread her fingers apart. "Five!"

1

"Yes, you're going to be five, and you're going to go to school this year too."

When she nodded, her light brown pigtails bobbed.

"But, if you leave, who's going to braid my hair?"

"Your mom can braid your hair."

"But, I like the way you do it. You do it better." Kelsey jumped up and down. "Will you braid my hair before you leave?"

"All right. One last time, and then I have to go." I knelt behind her, pulled the rubber bands off her pigtails, and braided her hair. I turned her around and kissed her forehead. "Now, you look beautiful."

Kelsey climbed up onto my bed and looked at herself in my dresser mirror. She turned her head several times, her braid swished back and forth, a smile spread across her face. "Thank you, Sandy."

Karen was my school counselor, and Dan was my tennis coach at Summit High School in Breckenridge, Colorado. Last January, shortly after my eighteenth birthday, my mother left me standing in the parking lot of our apartment building where we had lived for five months. Karen and Dan took me in and let me live with them until I graduated. Now, I had the freedom to go anywhere and be anyone I wanted to be. When I was just ten years old, I had freedom when my mother decided motherhood was not for her. She would leave me with my sister, who was only two years older, on Friday nights and not come home until Sunday night. But at that age, it wasn't freedom. It was more like abandonment. After my mother turned the corner and drove away, she never looked back, leaving *me* like a dog on the side of the road, left behind by an owner who didn't want it anymore. That was the day I was forced to become Sandy Kelly, who no longer belonged

2

to anyone, and I was determined not to be a dog left on the side of the road ever again.

I reached into my front pocket and pulled out my favorite strawberry lip gloss, removed the cap, swiped the wand across Kelsey's lips, and then closed it. Kelsey licked her lips and smiled.

I held my hand out. "Here, you can hold onto my lip gloss until I get home, okay?"

Kelsey nodded again with a smile. She rolled it back and forth in her hands and pushed it into her jeans pocket.

"I have to finish packing, Kelsey." I turned and searched the top of my dresser for anything else I might need for the trip. I grabbed another lip gloss, but I hesitated before sliding it into a side pocket next to my water bottle pouch. Glancing in the mirror, I brushed my light brown hair over one shoulder. I could see Kelsey watching me in the mirror behind me. A car horn honked twice, sending a shiver through my body.

I took a deep breath. *This is it.*

It was a great feeling to be on my own when you're young. No responsibilities and nobody telling you what to do, but then it was scary and sad at the same time. Sad because there was nobody to love you and nobody to love. A new chapter in my life was about to begin—kind of like a new chapter in a book. So, you kept reading to find out what happened.

"Sandy, Holly's here," Karen yelled from the living room.

"Coming." I picked up my graduation announcement and found a pewter guardian angel clip beneath it. The clip was inscribed "Daughter's Guardian Angel, please travel safely."

Kelsey walked to the edge of the bed. "What is that?"

"It's a guardian angel my stepmother gave me last year before I moved here. I guess she thought I needed a guardian angel—I think she was right." It was sad that my stepmother was more of a mother than my own. Not even my dad, who told me there was no room for me, seemed to care—but my stepmother did. But she had no power to change anything.

Kelsey reached up and ran her finger across my chin. "What happened there?"

"It's a scar." I tossed the angel clip inside my backpack, swung the bag over my shoulder, and waved to Holly through my bedroom window.

Kelsey started jumping on my bed. "How did you get it?"

"I got it when I was jumping on my bed, my sister pushed me, and I fell on the headboard. Um, maybe you shouldn't jump on the bed anymore." I lifted her and set her on the floor.

"Oh. Did it hurt?"

I laughed. "I was probably your age when it happened, so I don't remember."

Kelsey tugged on my shorts. "What's a stepmother?"

"Ah, a stepmother is like a second mother."

"Do I have a second mother?"

"No."

"Is my mother your second mother?"

"No, well, she's—maybe like my third."

"Wow, you have three mothers, and I only have one?"

"You only need one, and you have a great mother. Okay?" She nodded.

I never understood why my mother left that day. When I was younger, I thought the only way she would leave me was by dying of old age because mothers didn't just leave their children. Right? Silly me.

"I gotta go now, Kelsey." I took her hand and walked into the living room where Karen and Dan waited. Karen held out

4

a big bag of M&M's and a pack of strawberry Twizzlers. "I got these for your big trip out West. You're going to love all the national parks and especially San Diego. I'm jealous. I wish I were going with you and Holly."

"Thanks, Karen, but we need to go off on our own." *I need to find myself, and get away from people who don't love me or want me.* I wanted to appreciate the people who had stuck by me, and who cared, like Karen and Dan.

I always hoped I had someone to help me when I needed help, but I kept finding I had to do it alone. Karen and Dan offered me advice here and there, but really I could take it or leave it. Most of the time, I had taken it, but I didn't want to feel weak for not knowing how to do it by myself. Sometimes I pretended I didn't care. But I really did care. *I am not weak. I don't care anymore if my mother called me weak when I cried—she's gone so, she'll never see me cry again. Maybe one day I will be able to stand on my own two feet and take charge of myself and my life without anyone's help. But how? Where do I find the strength to be my own person? How do you find yourself when you don't know where to look and who to listen to?*

Karen opened the front door and pulled me close. "Now, be careful, and think before you do anything that will get you into trouble. I know you're going to have fun, and maybe you'll come back a changed young lady." Karen adjusted the strap on my backpack. "I know you told me several times, but how long will you be gone again?"

"I don't know, maybe until August or when our money runs out."

Karen's voice cracked. "Make sure you call me and let me know how you're doing."

"I will. Don't worry. And yes, before you ask, I have your phone number."

Dan laughed. "We'll be here if you need us. And have fun."

"Watch out for wild animals, and stay away from strange men, and—"

"I got it." Warmth spread through my body. *I know Karen and Dan care about me.* My voice softened. "I will. And I'll be okay."

Kelsey yanked my backpack. I kneeled. "Hey, Kels. Thanks for helping me pack."

She lunged forward, almost knocking me down, and wrapped her arms around me. Her eyes started to water. "I'm going to miss you."

"I'm going to miss you too."

Kelsey squeezed my waist. "I hope your angel keeps you safe."

I ran my hand over her braids. "Me too."

Dan and Karen stood at the door, and Kelsey peeked around her dad's leg. I waved goodbye, walking to Holly's dark-green 1975 Impala, tossed my backpack in the back seat and hopped in the front.

Holly and I met at gymnastics camp in Chicago four years before, and we'd been friends ever since. We borrowed each other's clothes and did everything together. I hadn't seen her since I had to leave Chicago the prior September. After I left, we only spoke on the phone.

Holly was born on October 13th; she was a Libra—an air sign. She was born on a Friday. Friday children were known to be loving and forgiving, obsessed with beauty and love. We shared the same green eye color. Holly was more diplomatic than me. She could say 'fuck off' without saying it, but I was the one who said it out loud. We were a perfect match for each other.

Holly smiled as she spoke. "Ready, girl?"

"Yep, let's go." It looked like Holly had grown her dark-brown hair out. When I left Chicago, her hair had been shoulder length. Now it was past her shoulders.

Holly motioned toward the back seat. "I've got a cooler for drinks and food in the back seat and the tent and sleeping bags and pillows in the trunk. We'll stop and grab more snacks when we fill the tank."

I held up the bag of M&M's and Twizzlers.

She high-fived me. "Nice."

"Do you think we'll need the tent?" I asked.

"Yep, we sure will. Hotels are way too expensive. It's going to be so cool camping out under the stars. By the way, how much money do you have?"

"I've got twelve-hundred."

"Good. I've got a little over one thousand and my mom gave me a gas card so we won't have to use our money for that. Where'd you get twelve hundred?"

"From the money my dad sent me for child support after my mom left. Dan made me put it all in a savings account. He wanted me to use it for school, but when I told him about going with you, he said it was okay to use it. I'm so glad he made me save it, or else I wouldn't be able to go. And then they gave me two hundred, plus a national park pass for graduation."

"That was pretty nice of them."

"Yeah, it was."

I reached behind me and pulled my journal out of my backpack. "Should we write our trip in a journal?"

"Hell no, I don't want anyone to know what we're going to do. It's nobody's business." She giggled. "I'm tired of people judging me and what I do or don't do." Then she winked at me.

I nodded my head slowly. "Yeah, me too." *What is she talking about? Holly has a better life than me. I'm used to people judging me, like teachers and people at school who don't know me. She must be joking...I think.* I pulled two more books out. "Dan gave me these books of the national parks and a book on California. There's a lot of cool things to do. I can't wait. *I'm going to see the world.* We are going to have so much fun. We have to drive around Hollywood and see if we can see any famous movie stars, like John Travolta or the Fonz, and, of course, we have to go see the Hollywood sign."

"And then we're going to climb mountains and swim in the ocean, and…."

"Meet boys and…" *Pretend we're someone else and get lost in a new life.*

🐱 🐱 🐱

After turning onto the main street, I pointed to the right. "Let's pull over and I'll show you what I've mapped out so far."

Holly pulled into the Super Saver shopping center, straddling two parking spots. I unfolded the road map, spread it across our laps, and traced my finger along a red line that Dan marked earlier. "This is our route. We'll head west into Utah, then south into Arizona, and over to California. Up along the coast, into Nevada, through Utah, and back home to Breckenridge."

"Okay, that makes sense. Where to first?"

I pointed on the map. "First stop, Arches National Park in Utah, which is two-hundred-ninety miles west."

I was born on January 18th, a Wednesday, which made me a Capricorn, an Earth sign, and a dull sea-goat. Wednesday children were versatile, very communicative, a bit careless, and most importantly, they were profound thinkers. I was a dreamer and a little bossy. My problem was, I was not a quick thinker. My thoughts and ideas often distracted me, causing me to overthink. I had an overactive imagination. It wasn't hard for me to come up with rational or irrational reasons for why people said what they did and how they acted. Because of my mother, I questioned everything in my life, and I had no patience for liars, backstabbers, users, and fakers.

Was I not pretty enough, or not smart enough, or was I just not enough for my mother to love me? I took a deep breath and let it out slowly. *I'm not going to let her ruin me.* Somehow, I believed miracles could happen, and someday they would come true. But I had no idea what miracle I wanted. I thought I'd only get one miracle in my life because I didn't think I was good enough to get more than one. So, I didn't want to waste it on something I could achieve myself.

Maybe when I'm older, I'll write a book with all the thoughts in my head and discover through my own words what the secret to happiness is. Life is hard. This trip will be the end of the old me, and I'm okay with that.

Holly glanced at the gas gauge on the instrument panel. "Maybe I should fill the car up before we leave." We drove down the road and pulled into the gas station.

"I'm going to run inside and grab a few things. I'll be right back," I said.

"Get some Hawaiian Punch while you're in there," Holly yelled after me.

After looking around the store, I pulled five dollars out of my pocket and laid it on the counter next to a six-pack of Hawaiian Punch and a bag of Fritos. As the store clerk reached for my money, I couldn't help but notice his long, gray fingernails. They matched his long, gray hair, which looked as gray as my pewter guardian angel.

"How are you, young lady?" he asked, smiling down at me.

A shiver ran through my body. "Um, good."

"Where are you and your friend off to?" He tilted his head toward the window where Holly pumped gas.

My eyes lifted to meet his eyes. I followed his nod. "We're heading west to some national parks, and then into California." *Oh no, maybe I should have told him we were going east.*

He handed me my change. I quickly counted it and shoved it into my pocket.

"Are you girls running away?"

My heart shuddered. I glanced up. The image of my mother running away flashed in my head. *Maybe I'm running away too. No, no, I'm not running away! I will not be like her!*

"Ah, no, we're not running away. It's… it's just a summer vacation."

His eyes held a light. "Okay, a finding yourself trip?" he asked whimsically.

"What?" I stared into his eyes. Even they were gray, they had a softness to them. How would this total stranger even know what I was doing?

"I traveled the world when I was younger. And every once in a while, I'd get an itch to take off to figure out what life was about and where I fit in. So, you can call it whatever you want, but I think you're looking for something...." He pointed out the window. "Out there. You know not all who wander are lost. Sometimes you find yourself."

His words ran through my head. *I guess I'm looking for something, but I just don't know what I should be looking for.*

He cleared his throat. "So, while you're out there exploring and finding the meaning of life and what it holds for you or whatever you're looking for, make sure you take some time along the way and look for some geodes." His eyes twinkled.

My eyebrows rose. "What's a geode?"

His eyes twinkled. "You've never seen a geode?"

"No...." My voice cracked with curiosity.

He smiled. "A nodule?"

I tucked a strand of hair behind my ear. "No...."

He leaned forward. His voice lowered. "Well, let me tell you, sweetheart, geodes, and nodules are one of nature's secrets. They look like any other ordinary round rocks, and when you crack a geode open, the hollow cavities have the most beautiful quartz crystals you've ever seen." A smile flashed across his lips. He rested his elbows on the counter. His hands, rough and wrinkled, unfolded open as he talked. "Some have sparkling jagged amethyst. Some are white, and if you find one with black crystals, those are very rare."

I leaned back, picturing his words. "What is the other one you mentioned?"

"Oh, the nodules. They look the same on the outside, except the nodules are solid and flat inside and very colorful." His fingers circled on the counter. "Minerals that have settled over thousands of years form colored rings and swirls inside."

"Where do you find those?"

He pointed out the window. "They're out West. You'll find them anywhere there's rock debris from erosion. Look in riverbeds where water has washed them from broken mountains after heavy rains." He leaned closer; his voice lowered. "But the cool thing is the secrets they hold inside… kind of like the secrets we hold inside ourselves." He winked. "Find those, and you'll find what you're looking for."

I straightened my back and stepped away. He slid my Hawaiian Punch and Fritos across the counter to me. "You'll know what I'm talking about when you see it and feel it." He walked around the counter and pulled a few brochures from a wood rack by the door. "Here's some information about the national parks. Take in all the nature and beauty around you. Breathe it in, and…."

My mind trailed off as he spoke. The inside of my stomach fluttered. *I want a geode.*

The bell to the door chimed, and a woman behind me asked, "How do you get to Vail from here?" The gray man stepped toward the window, pointing, giving her directions. A beam of light shining in surrounded him in a way that looked like a halo around his head. The back of my neck tingled. I backed out of the door without him finishing about breathing in and…I wanted to hear more about the geodes.

"Hey, what took you so long?" Holly yelled out the window.

I opened the car door and slid in. "Oh, this guy was telling me about geodes and nodules. He seemed kinda creepy when he was talking, but I'm kinda interested in what they are."

"What the heck are geo and nod-who?"

"Some kind of rocks that you break open, and I guess they have crystals and rings inside."

"And where do we find these geod…?"

"Geodes. He said you could find them in the desert or out West. I'm going to try and find one." I wanted to see what was so unique and beautiful inside a plain old rock that lay beneath dirt and debris. And of course, I was curious to know what the secrets inside those rocks were. Could the secret to happiness be inside a rock?

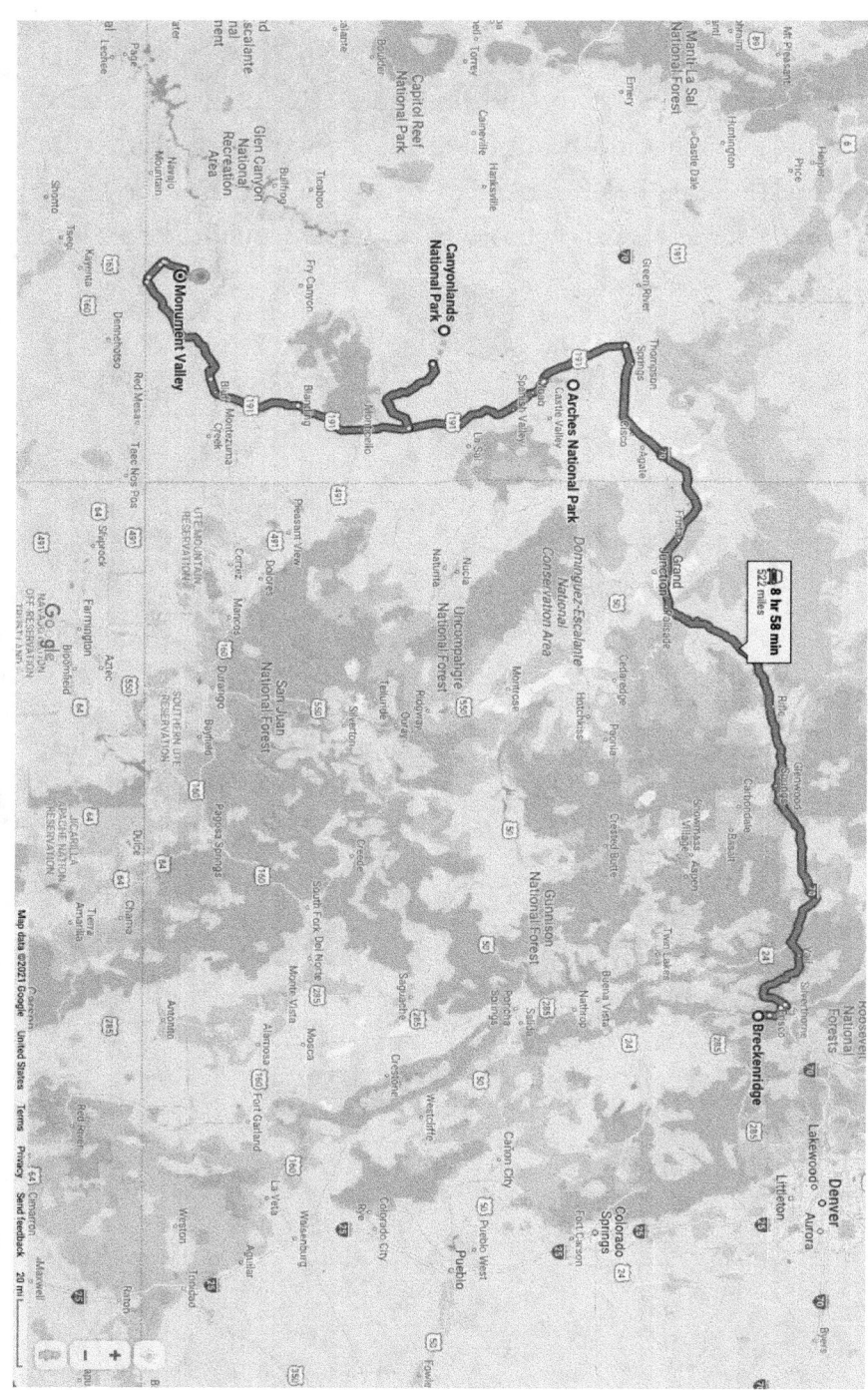

TWO

Do You Know Where You're Going To?

Before we headed west on I-70, we passed the familiar streets of Breckenridge. I gazed out the window, and looked down the streets where Clarissa, Jason, and, of course JD McCarron, the three closest high school friends I had in Breckenridge lived. So many times, I thought about JD and me together again. He was my first...uhm...love. It was hard to forget. He was hard to forget. But I'd never say it out loud. *I wonder if they're home and can see me driving away, off to see the world with my best friend. Well, maybe not the world, but the West at least. I bet they're in Cabo, traveling in Europe or some exotic island like they used to go to in the summers and on spring break before they head off to college. I wonder if JD still thinks about me.* Trees blurred as we drove past but the memories of parties and football games were clear. My friends from Breckenridge were still very fresh in my mind. I could hardly remember my old friends from Chicago. Those days seemed so far away—even Holly, even though she was right there with me in the car.

We entered I-70 West, leaving the many original historic buildings and facades along the main street that took you back to when Breckenridge was part of a Wild West mining town. Now, clothing stores and ski rental outfitters had taken over with cowboy boots, hats, artwork, handmade trinkets, and soaps dressing the window fronts.

Two-hundred and eighty-nine miles to Arches National Park, Utah. The arches were known as the Red Rock Wonderland. Golden grasses along the side of the road waved in the breeze as we passed by. Barbed-wire fencing stretched for miles along the road. Clouds rolled in and out, casting shadows along the open landscape. The radio blared our favorite songs while Holly and I sang and sipped Hawaiian Punch.

Growing up, my family didn't travel much. However, a few times a year, my family and grandparents drove to my great-grandparents' house in Rock Falls, Illinois. It was only a two-hour drive, but it felt more like seven. I sat in the back seat of my grandmother's Buick and stared at the floating ball in the compass mounted on the dashboard. Then, before it hypnotized me, I'd look out the side window and watch the highway signs zoom by.

Signs told the driver it was okay to 'pass with care' and how fast to drive. I remembered the nervous feeling I'd get when many cars passed us on the left, worrying if they would get around us before another one would come in the other direction. Often, I would close my eyes until the car passed, hoping that I'd still be alive when I opened my eyes. Many cars passed us, because my grandfather was a very slow driver. He was never in a hurry to do anything and was always busy doing something around the house. Grandpa would always wear dark-blue one-piece coveralls and thick work gloves before heading off for a day of work, either fixing things, cleaning, chopping wood, or gardening. He always shooed us grandkids away when he was working and didn't want us around.

16

One day unexpectedly, my grandmother told me she never really loved him. My childhood rose colored glasses cracked for the first time. I never thought of my grandmother the same way after that day. I thought she loved everyone. I was wrong. My grandpa was a good man, regardless of what my grandmother said about him. After that day, knowing my grandfather was in a loveless marriage made me more determined not to be somewhere I wasn't loved or wanted again. I hated my grandmother for saying that, and I hated her even more when she told me I wasn't her favorite grandchild. I guess people can hide their true feelings well.

As we got closer to Utah, we saw black, white, and painted horses running free across the open fields in the distance. Their wind-swept manes floated in the air behind them, the earth kicked up by their hooves.

I rolled the window down and rested my head on the door. "Look, Holly, see the horses?"

"Where'd they come from?"

"Those are wild horses. I've heard stories that there's a lot of them out here, but I've never seen them."

"So, who would the horses belong to? Anyone?"

"They belong to nobody. They're just free." I watched them out my window running in a herd as they sprinted in one direction and then turned, disappearing into the grasslands. They were soldiers in their *own* army. Their quest was to not get fenced in, and to keep moving forward. I envisioned myself running with them, wind flowing through my hair, my spirit free.

"Whatcha thinking about?" Holly asked.

I answered without taking my eyes off the last of the horses fading in the distance. "Tom."

"Cowboy Tom?" Holly giggled.

"Yep. Cowboy Tom."

After JD broke up with me, I dated Tom Carrillo. JD hated Tom. So, I dated Tom—just to make JD jealous. His family owned a horse ranch on Breckenridge's outskirts, and we went riding whenever we could.

I loved riding on top of an independent, spirited animal. My hands held the reins tight. My horse jogged, trotted, cantered, and galloped, taking me along on his journey. Tom's father said there's an old saying that "All horses will trust a good leader, and all horses are capable of trusting someone in their lives."

"Hey, do you ever think about JD?" Holly asked.

A smile tugged at my lips and then faded. I turned away from the window. "Yeah…sorta." When I moved to Breckenridge, I met JD McCarron. He stole my heart. He loved me and showed me how to love. He took something that I could never give another—and then, he left me.

"Have you talked to him lately?"

"No." *Maybe, sometimes.* "I haven't talked to him or seen him since graduation. He invited me to his graduation party, but I didn't go. He's going to the University of Colorado in Boulder in August."

"Maybe we'll make it back before he leaves."

A heavy sigh escaped. *I would love to see him again.* "I'm good. I don't need to say goodbye to him." *I said goodbye when he dumped me for Cabo girl. So why do I keep thinking about him?*

A few hours down the highway, we stopped at a gas station, stretched our legs, and I tossed our Hawaiian Punch cans in the trash.

"People do change, ya know," Holly said while pumping gas.

I glanced over at her. "Who are you talking about?"

18

"I'm talking about JD."

"Why?"

"He wanted you back, didn't he?"

"Yeah, but—"

"But nothing. People do change. Especially when they realize they lost someone they loved."

Not everyone changes. But I wish some would.

Yes, people change, and so have I. And, why is Holly pushing me to get back with JD? Doesn't she remember how he broke my heart when he broke up with me so he could fool around with the Cabo girl on spring break?

The warm summer air flowed through the four rolled-down windows as we drove down the highway. I grabbed a handful of M&M's and popped them in my mouth. The candy shell cracked, and the warm chocolate coated my tongue. I turned and looked at Holly. "So, anyone interesting in your life?" *After you went out with my old boyfriend from back home after I left?*

Holly squirmed. "Ah, no. After Rusty and I broke up, I wanted to take a break."

I swallowed hard. "Were you really going to marry Rusty?"

She looked over at me. "Why?"

"Ah…"

She reached over and nudged my arm. "Don't worry. No. I like him a lot. You know what he's like. He's a better friend than a boyfriend. So, when he asked me, I kinda felt bad saying no. But, he was holding a diamond ring and looked so happy, so I said yes. I didn't want to hurt him."

For the first time, it was silent in the car.

I shook my head, and I laughed. Holly laughed too.

"Besides, I couldn't marry your ex-boyfriend." She emphasized 'ex.' "So, I had to tell him that I wasn't ready to get married and gave his ring back."

"Oh, sure, blame it on me. It wouldn't have mattered if you wanted to marry Rusty. He was my old boyfriend, and that was a long time ago." *I can't hold on to all my old boyfriends— can I?*

I didn't think their marriage would have worked out anyway. I started picturing flower petals dropping to the ground. Holly and Rusty walking down the aisle of tall grasses in an open meadow, so in love. Me, following behind, wearing an ugly pink taffeta dress, and holding wilted daisies. *I don't like pink.* Holly's beautiful white lace and tulle dress floating in the spring air. Baby's breath weaved into her long dark hair, cascading over her shoulders. Everyone smiled and clapped as the happy couple walked by. And then there was me, smiling at the cameras, but deep down inside, I wanted to beat them both with my lifeless, wilted bouquet. But I wasn't jealous or angry. I was where everyone could see me, but everyone was there for Holly—not me. *Nobody's here for me.*

Holly rested her hand on my arm. "Yes, it would have mattered because I care more about you than him."

Maybe I won't beat them with my beautiful flowers. "Thanks, Holly."

"We're too young to get serious with anyone anyway."

"You're so right." *I don't ever want to marry someone just for a ring and then later say I never loved them. I guess relationships and friendships can erode over time, and feelings for one another can wash away. Sometimes you hang on and sometimes you let go—but how do you let go?*

20

THREE

Arches Are Hollow Strength

Erosion is the geological process in which earthen materials are worn away and transported by natural forces such as wind or water. — National Geographic.

The sign on the road said, "Welcome to Utah. The Mormon State." It took us four hours and thirty minutes to get here. My legs fell asleep a few times even though I had stretched them out on the dashboard several times. Utah houses five national parks: Arches, Canyonland, Bryce Canyon, Capitol Reef, and Zion National Park.

Our first stop was Arches National Park, home of the natural arches. Seven dollars a night to camp, but no showers.

The Arches map at the kiosk showed the many trails and directions to various natural red sandstone arches.

I yelled over to Holly, who was double knotting her shoelaces against a rock. "There's, like, over nine-hundred arches here."

"We don't have much time to see them all today," Holly yelled back.

"Okay, let's go to the Delicate Arch first. It's the most popular and the largest freestanding arch in the park. The map says it's fifty-two feet high, and it's only a three-mile round trip to get there." *I can do that, no problem.*

We smeared sunscreen over our exposed skin before our hike, grabbed our water bottles, backpacks, and tied our shoelaces in double knots. For at least an hour, we hiked along on the smooth slide rock incline, following a trail of other explorers trudging in the hot sun with no shade in sight. The blistering sun dried our sweat-soaked tank tops to our skin. Several people in front of us stopped to rest and drank from their water bottles under small Juniper trees along the trail. Minutes later, we approached a man fanning his partner, breathing heavily, leaning against a tree, her hand tugging at her clothing. A young man nearby yelled to him, "I'll go find help. Keep giving her water."

I stopped beside them. "Do you need help?"

The man held a water bottle to his partner's lips. "I think she's just overheated. Someone's going to get help." He glanced over at Holly and me. "Make sure you girls have enough water. It's awfully hot out today."

I held my water bottle tight. "We have enough water," I yelled back.

We soldiered on, holding on to our water bottles for dear life. The trail narrowed further up the incline, a steep rock wall on one side and a steep drop-off on the other. Small rocks and dirt tumbled under our feet when we walked, causing us to slip and slide on the trail. There was no railing or room for error if we stumbled and fell. Falling would surely mean death. At every turn, there were so many ways you could die. Fall off a cliff, get mauled by a bear or mountain lion, or even die of thirst. *I'm not going to die today. I'm not going to die today.* Hikers passed in the other direction, and I found myself hugging a sandstone wall. I started planning my funeral. *This arch better be worth it.* We turned the corner, the path opened. Seconds later, the red, twisted freestanding arch stood before us, backdropped by the deep dark blue sky that went on forever like nothing I'd ever seen before. The arch looked like something you could mold out of red modeling clay. *This arch is unbelievable. I wonder why they call it the Delicate Arch? It looks so strong, not delicate to me at all. This hike was so worth it.*

"Oh, my God, Holly, can you believe this?" I was in awe of how small I was standing face to face in nature in its purest form.

"It's amazing. Let's get closer," Holly said.

We crossed the slick red-rock floor leading to the giant red twisted arch.

"How old is this arch?" Holly asked.

"I'd guess a gazillion years old." I took my eyes off the arch and scanned the solid rock floor for anything that could be a geode. There were no rocks, only red dust that occasionally blew in the soft hot air.

If erosion can create this beautiful arch, then erosion can't be that bad. It looks like something beautiful can emerge from destruction and stand strong even though it's hollow inside, nothing supporting it except time. Maybe I could be an arch someday. No. I will be an arch someday.

After a few more hours of hiking to the many arches, we got back to the car as the sun was starting to set. We drove down the road to the Teetering Giant Balanced Rock. The large red-rock formation balancing on a narrow rock pedestal glowed in the orange sun setting against a purplish sky.

"I don't think that rock is really balancing on top, do you Holly?" I walked around to the other side. *Could this be a giant geode?* "I think it's attached to the rock pedestal below, somehow."

"That pedestal looks pretty fragile. I can't believe that is all that is holding it up. How long will it take before that rock comes crashing down?"

"I don't know. It's kinda scary. Let's not get too close. It could fall any minute." *Nope, I'm staying far enough away in case it decides to fall.* "You saw how many trails were closed because of falling rocks, didn't you?"

"Where is your sense of adventure?" Holly teased.

"I left it back at the car. I don't want it to get crushed." *This rock is just so crazy how it's just balanced on top.* I took a step back. *Safety first.* "It's magnificent, though."

We pulled into Devil's Garden Campground a few miles down the road, where we tent camped for the next three nights. There were many other tent campers and RVs around our campsite. Once we finally got our tent up, after several tries, we settled in listening to Beatles songs on radios in the distance, one piece of music after another. Reggae music thumped on and off next to us. "Eleanor Rigby" with a reggae vibe sounded cool. *Ha, I remember singing "Eleanor Rigby" in grade school. The music teacher must have been a Beatles fan.* We were all different, and yet we all enjoyed the same things: nature and music.

We laid with our heads out of the tent. Our legs ached, and our feet ached. The cool desert breeze brushed against our suntanned faces. When I closed my eyes, I thought about JD. *I wonder if he has changed and still thinks about me.*

Later that night, coyotes yapped at the moon, lulling me to sleep under the glittering stars above.

In the morning, we dressed in tank tops, shorts, and tennis shoes. We slathered on sunscreen and wrapped bandanas around the tops of our heads. My bandana was blue and white, and Holly's was purple and white.

We hiked along the twisting paths in the Devil's Garden to more arches. The hike started out on hard packed flat dirt with only slight hills up and down. We even saw people with strollers walking the trail. When Holly and I stopped to rest. I pulled the book of the national parks out of my pack. I looked up and pointed. "This is the Landscape Arch. It's the longest slightly oval natural sandstone arch in North America." I turned the page. "The arch hangs by a very thin fragile thread, which is only six feet thick." It looked like stretched out taffy before it broke away.

"This is the thinnest arch we've seen so far. Hey, are you still looking at that book?" Holly asked.

"Um...yes."

"Put it away, and let's just go and see what we see."

I flipped through the pages. It said nothing about putting the book away. I slid the book into the side pocket of my backpack. "All right. You win. No more books. Let's go where the trail takes us."

Back on the trail, a few minutes later, we were climbing a rock section with steep drops on both sides.

Red, yellow, and white wildflowers added pops of color to the vast red sandstone down the trailhead. Every time we came upon a dried-up riverbed, I kicked at the dirt to unearth rocks and anything that would resemble what a geode could look like. I picked up several rocks, examined them in the sunlight, and ran my fingers over the hard surface, feeling for any cracks. I shook them, listening for rattling inside. I doubted any of them were geodes.

After a brief rest and a water break, we found Pine Tree Arch. It was a large ground-level arch, and pine trees grew at the base.

The Tunnel Arch was next. On top, it looked like a giant red stone bridge with a hole inside that you could crawl into.

After the Tunnel Arch, we found ourselves back on slick rock trails, scrambling over narrow rock ledges, and climbing over boulders to The Double O Arch. The Double O Arch was one full-circle arch stacked on a smaller oval arch. Both were part of the same sandstone fin. The lower arch was large enough to walk through.

We were hot, stinky, and almost out of water at the end of the trail. We headed back to the car before our water ran out, and we died of thirst. I continued to search for geodes under most of the sagebrush bushes along the trailhead, but only found broken slide rock. *There has to be at least one geode out here.*

We got back to the car and, before sunset, drove into the town of Moab. We bought sandwiches, sodas, ice, and snacks for lunches and dinners for the next few days. While Holly paid and gassed up, I found a phone in the back of the store to call Karen.

The phone rang several times. The answering machine picked up.

"Hey, Karen, it's Sandy. You guys must not be home. Anyway, we made it to Arches yesterday, and we're leaving in the morning. It's so beautiful here. The arches are amazing, and the Delicate Arch was massive. Before we left, some guy at the store told me to look for geodes and nodules while we're out here. Do you know what they are? I hope I find a bunch of them, or, well, a few would be good, but I'd be happy if I could find just one. We're off to Monument Valley in the morning, and if it's not too far out of the way, we'll stop by Canyonlands. Oh, by the way, Karen, your answering machine message isn't on. It doesn't say you've reached

Karen or Dan. It just says to leave a message. I'll call you in a day or two. Miss you guys."

FOUR

Cowboys Make the West Taste Good

In the morning, we headed down Highway 191 to Monument Valley, Utah. The campground was full service with running showers. I was so looking forward to having hot water pour over me and wash the red dirt and dust off. On the way there, we took a detour into Canyonlands, forty miles away. We hiked and spent about an hour gazing into the canyon mazes below. Another landscape created by erosion that hadn't changed in thousands of years, unlike my hometown of Chicago. In the city, change is good. New buildings, new businesses, apartments, and houses. New and exciting places to visit. Change transforms the town, making it exciting to live there. But the beauty of the unchanging landscape shows a simpler life out here. Nobody cares what brand of clothes you wear or if you're drinking a Starbucks Frappuccino.

I drove while Holly took a nap. My mind soared as I drove down the highway, passing farmland, ranches, and vast expanses of nothing. *I guess erosion is not all bad when something beautiful is left behind. There's so many beautiful arches left to see out here. But personal erosion can be sad and devastating. By the end of this trip, I hope I'll find out who I am and find my power.*

After driving another two hours and fifty minutes, we arrived at Monument Valley, known for freestanding natural red-rock buttes, set in the Navajo Tribal Park. It was only five dollars each to camp.

We drove the seventeen-mile Tribal Park loop. The red dust kicked up as we followed cars around the monuments. Holly parked on the side of the road and we walked the flat, soft, loose sand and rocks of the Wildcat Trail, which circled three miles around two large red sandstone buttes. Hiking the trail was like stepping back in time into the Wild West.

The first buttes we came to jutted up from the red desert floor were named East Mitten and West Mitten—like the left and right mittens on your hands. Next was The Merrick Butte. It was a massive square block of red sandstone up on a hill sloping to the vast flat red earth.

The same rust colored dust covered our sneakers as we walked, and the earthy scent of the red dirt hit our noses. *Thank God I brought my black sneakers.* The sun-blasted sky hung over us. There were no trees or bushes to shade us along this trail, just red dirt, and buttes, but we toughed it out. By now, we were used to the one-hundred-degree heat that had been beating down on us every day. Further down the trail, barking dogs warned us to stay away from the homes and property of the people who lived inside the park.

Holly drove down the main 'and only' road to the View Hotel, which was the only hotel in this valley. The Navajo Indians built the View Hotel and still owned it. After parking, we walked in and pretended that we belonged there. Navajo statues and rugs blanketed the floors and decorated the walls. In the center of the room, worn leather couches and chairs surrounded the center stone fireplace, above which hung a traditional Navajo headdress. It was like a museum. In the middle of the room, puzzle pieces lay on a rustic wood and metal table for guests to put together. It must cost a fortune to stay here.

We found the gift shop and searched for souvenirs. I scanned through a rack of photographs of monuments, buttes, cowboys, and sunsets. After looking at how much they cost, I decided our cameras' pictures were good enough. A light shining on a deep purple object sparkled in the light along the back wall. I hurried over. The sign below read "Geodes from around the world." *Oh, my God, is this a…geode? So, this is what the creepy gray guy was talking about.* A yellow citrine rock sat next to it. I measured by my hand. Both were about two feet tall and about eight inches wide. I turned to see where Holly was. She was at a glass cabinet looking at turquoise rings and necklaces. I took a few steps in her direction and motioned to her. "Holly, come quick."

"What did you find?" she asked walking toward me.

I grabbed her hand. "I think I found a geode."

She followed me to the back wall, and I pointed to the weathered wood shelf where the stones glittered under bright lights. "These are geodes." I ran my finger over the jagged crystal edges inside the cavity of the rock. "Look how beautiful they are."

"Yeah, they are beautiful, but look how much they cost. This purple one is twelve hundred, and the yellow one is nine hundred and fifty," Holly said.

"Why do they cost so much?"

"I guess because people will pay whatever they have to if they want one."

I'll never be able to afford one. I pointed to the right of the geodes. "And these flat ones are nodules. They're so pretty

31

too." I finally found a geode, but I couldn't afford it. *Ugh, I guess I'll never have a geode unless I find one myself.*

Holly tugged my arm. "Someday, you'll get one. Let's go check out the rest of the hotel."

"Wait one minute. I want to grab a few brochures for the places we were going to next and buy a postcard to send to Karen, since she's not answering her phone." Before I left the gift shop, I looked back at the geodes. *Maybe someday.* I wrote a quick message to Karen and Dan and popped the card in the mailbox at the front desk.

On a windless night, we relaxed in Adirondack chairs on the back patio of the hotel. We sipped Diet Cokes and stared out at the buttes in the distance. The evening sun melted behind the earth, leaving streaks of purple and orange hanging low in the sky until the sun completely disappeared. At night, the hotel played old John Wayne movies filmed in Monument Valley against one of its outside walls. Looking out across the valley, I imagined horse hooves beating the ground, the animals breathing heavily through flared nostrils, pulling Conestoga wagons. The wagons swayed side to side as they circled the red-rock formations, trying to escape the warpainted Native American Indians stampeding not far behind them. Seconds later, buff bandana-wearing hunky cowboys fired six-guns in the air and scared off the Indians. One of them could be my hero. Maybe one of them could save me. If I was in the wagon, I'd jump and run to one, or maybe both. I'd stretch onto my tiptoes, pull their bandanas down, and kiss them softly on their rough, wind-dried lips.

Later that evening, Holly and I set up our tent at the campsite down the road, then we drove back to the hotel, bought a couple of Diet Cokes and popcorn, and snuck out onto the patio. The movie *Rio Grande* was playing on the wall.

I glanced out into the darkness across the valley during the movie and wondered what my cowboy was doing. *I wonder if JD could have been my cowboy and I let him get away. But aren't cowboys supposed to save you, not hurt you?*

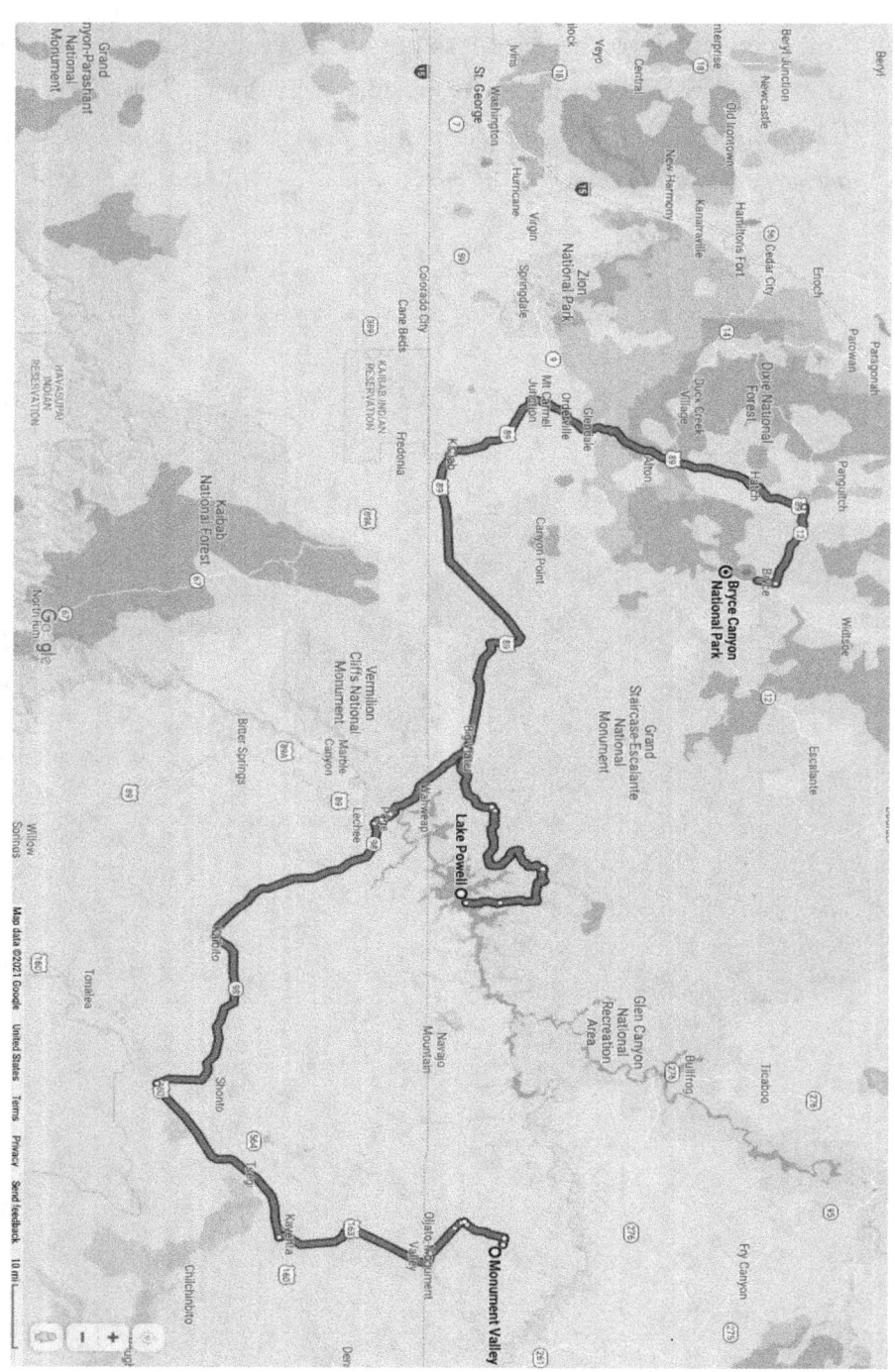

34

FIVE

It's Okay to be Fearful

The next morning, we ate untoasted blueberry frosted Pop-Tarts and then left Monument Valley. We headed south on Highway 163 and then northwest on Highway 98 to Lake Powell.

"Welcome to Lake Powell," the brochure read. "A man-made reservoir surrounded by canyon walls and towering vistas."

Holly parked the car and we took turns holding a towel around each other to change into our swimsuits. Then, we hiked along a short path to a swimming cove surrounded by smooth pinkish sandstone rock plateaus and cliff walls. We dropped our towels and submerged our sweaty bodies in the glassy, cool, calm water. When we came up for air, a few guys were jumping off a cliff near us.

"Ready for a little adventure?" Holly asked, swimming over to a flat ledge leading to the cliff.

I followed her up the side of the cliff that was a few stories high, navigating the smooth slick slide rock. "I'll jump if you jump."

"Deal," Holly answered, sliding behind me and pushing me up the rock.

At the top, I walked to the edge. "Ah…I think you should go first… If you survive, then I'll go."

Holly looked over the edge, then backed away, taking a few deep breaths. "All right, here I go." She took three running steps and jumped. Holly screamed out on her way down, her arms swung in the air before she plunged into the lake and disappeared underneath a splash of water. When her head popped above the surface, she shouted, "That was awesome!"

I watched her below.

"It's your turn. You can do it, girl. You'll love it," Holly yelled.

My feet slid along the warm rock to the edge.

"Hurry up. People are waiting," Holly yelled from below.

I turned around. "One minute." I began the countdown. I breathed in deeply. "One…Two…Three…Go."

I didn't move. I peeked over the edge where Holly was treading water, waiting for me. *She's so brave.*

"Go, girl."

"All right, all right. This time for sure." *You can do this. Be brave, be strong. Be an arch.* I turned and looked at the people standing behind me, waiting for their turn. "Do you want to go first?"

"Nope, it's your turn. We'll wait," the two dripping-wet guys behind me said.

My heart pounded like a drum as my toes hugged the edge. I took a deep breath and let it out. "Ready…Go…" I shut my eyes tight, and power jumped. Hands high above my head. For a few short seconds, I fell through the air. Butterflies fluttered in my stomach. I held my breath as my feet hit the water. The chilly water sent shivers through my body as it rushed over me the further I sank. *Oh, my God, I did*

36

it. I jumped; I lived. I scrambled my way to the surface. People on the cliff clapped. My cheeks reddened. *Oh, my God, I loved it!* I shouted like a pro over to Holly. "Let's do it again."

"I knew you could do it."

I jumped a few more times with no hesitation and no more clapping from the spectators. About an hour later, we found a beach and dried off in the sun. We ate lunch and sipped Hawaiian Punch through our stale Twizzlers.

I scanned the lake, the cliffs, a few boats on the water, and then focused on the few clouds hanging in the sky. "Hey, Holly, can you imagine living here? We could swim and jump off the cliffs every day."

"Yep, that would be nice. Other than here, where do you think we should live now that we are free to do what we want?"

"I don't know. It would be nice living here, but where would we work or live? And it doesn't look like there's much to do here either. Besides, I need a little more action in my life. Everywhere we've been so far was nice and beautiful, but I need more...I need something more. And where the hell are all these geodes at?"

"You need to forget about the stupid geodes."

"They aren't stupid. You saw how beautiful they are."

"Yeah, but I don't think you're going to find one...out here."

"I know. I've looked everywhere, and I haven't found one."

"I don't think you looked everywhere," Holly laughed.

I'll find one, one of these days. My mind wandered back to the creepy gas station guy. "Creepy gray guy was so sure about the secret inside."

"And what is the big secret anyway?" Holly asked.

"I don't know."

Holly sighed. "I don't want you to be disappointed if you don't find what you're looking for. I think the creepy guy lied to you about the secrets they hold inside. Maybe there's no secret after all. Maybe it's what you want to believe in."

"I'll find the secret someday."

"Sometimes, someday never comes."

"What?"

"Never mind. Hey, are you still going to live in Colorado when you get home?" Holly asked.

"Yeah. I love Colorado and the mountains. I mean, I still miss home and you, but I've been in Colorado for a year now, and I want to stay, but I need to figure out what I want to do when I get home."

"Well, when I get home, I'm not sure I'll stay in Chicago. Maybe I won't even go back."

I turned to face her. "Really?"

"Yep."

"Where would you go?"

"I want to go somewhere warm, somewhere exciting."

All I want is to go where the geodes are.

At the gas station, I called Karen, and got her answering machine again. "Hey, Karen, it's Sandy. So many cool things out here. We had enough time to stop at Canyonlands. The canyons were massive, and they went on forever. It's hard to believe that land was formed like this—so many different colors layered in the rock. And then at Monument Valley, I swear this is what Mars could look like. Barren red sandy dirt with rock formations and buttes expanded out in the horizon—not a tree in sight. It was like being on another planet. It's been so hot during the day, but at night, it cools off enough to sleep. Today we stopped at Lake Powell and went swimming. The water was kinda cold, but we got used to it. Have you and Dan ever been to Lake Powell? I'm sure you have. You guys have been everywhere. Anyway, Holly talked me into cliff jumping. I was so scared at first, but I finally jumped. I guess if the fear doesn't go away, I'll have to do everything afraid. I finally found some geodes, except they were in the gift shop at the View Hotel, in Monument Valley. They were so beautiful, and expensive. I still want to find my own geode. One that will have meaning because I found it, and I'll never forget how I got it. So, I'll keep looking. Tomorrow we are off to Bryce Canyon and then the Grand Canyon. Talk to you later. Oh, and your voicemail still isn't set up yet. Miss you guys."

I wondered why Karen wasn't answering the phone. *She's always home. Why isn't she there?*

SIX

Spirits, Good or Bad, Mystery or Myth

Welcome to Bryce Canyon National Park, Utah. Known for phantom-like rock spires, hoodoos, fluted walls, and sculptured pinnacles. All were created by erosion thousands of years ago.

"Did you see the sign, Holly? This park has showers." *Yay.*

We parked and walked to the information map and trailhead kiosk.

"Let's hike the Fairyland Loop. It says it has great views of the amphitheater and hoodoos. Whatever those are. And it's only eight miles. We can do that easily. But we need to fill up our water bottles first."

We could see the red, pink, and jagged yellow peaks of rock formations from the top of the trail. The further we walked down the trail, the more the colors changed in the shadows as the light turned to dark and the dark changed to light. Dark red replaced pink and yellow. The brilliant green bushes and native trees contrasted beautifully against the red rock. A mile down the trail, we approached a man and woman wearing matching khaki hiking shorts, boots, hats, and windbreakers tied around their waists.

"The hoodoos are breathtaking," the woman said to the man.

I stepped closer to see what they were looking at. "Excuse me, what's a hoodoo?"

The woman's eyes lit up. She extended her arms out around her. "This sea of red sandstone rock formations are hoodoos. When the rain and snow freeze and then thaw, over time, the freezing and thawing split and carve through the rock. That's how the hoodoos are formed—making it look like creatures with faces huddled together."

The man lowered his binoculars. His thick glasses framed his whimsical eyes. "The hoodoos come alive when the sun sets on them." He raised his hand and wiggled his fingers toward the sky. "And late in the day when the clouds roll over the hoodoos, the hoodoos come out and dance in the shade." His smile never left his face.

The woman stepped closer to Holly and me. She lowered her head, casting a shadow on our feet from the brim of her REI explorer hat. "There's an urban myth that hoodoos were formed when a God named Coyote turned the Legend people to stone for taking more than their share of the water and pine nuts from the land."

The woman scanned the serene, jagged rock amphitheater of hoodoos that seemed to go on for miles high and low. "If you listen closely, you can hear the hoodoos whispering in the wind."

My stomach quivered. "Oh, okay, thanks." I reached back and grabbed Holly's arm. "Are you ready to go, Holly?" I backed away, pulling her with me.

The woman shouted. "You have to look deep into the hoodoos to see their faces, and then you'll feel their spirit."

A few steps away, Holly asked, "You're not scared of hoodoos, are you?"

My skin tingled. "No! Keep walking. I scrambled past Holly. "Are you coming? Because I'm not leaving without you, and you're not leaving without me."

"I'm coming."

Farther down the loop, I stopped and scanned the hoodoos. "Holly, do you believe that hoodoo stuff?"

"I don't know. She said it was a myth, right? Do you believe it?"

"I don't know either. But I… Did you hear that?"

"What?"

"Shhhhh…that…it was like a whistling noise."

Air swirled around us. Red dirt danced around our feet and then floated away as quickly as it came.

Holly stepped closer to me. "It's just the wind…I think."

I turned and looked around the amphitheater of hoodoos. I tried to make out faces in the eroded rock formations. "That's what that woman said. You can hear the hoodoos talk when the wind blows."

The wind blew past again. This time it was a hissing noise. I grabbed Holly's arm. "I think they're talking again."

"What are they saying now?"

"I think they're saying we should leave." I hurried down the trail.

Holly followed behind me. "They may not be bad spirits, you know. They could be good ones, silly girl."

"When I think of spirits, I think of ghosts who come and haunt you."

"Well, let's pretend these are good spirits. Spirits that warn you of bad things to come. Like spirits that will watch over

43

us. Or maybe these spirits are trying to tell you where all the geodes are." She snickered.

I was a few feet in front of Holly. I quickly turned, raised my arms, and yelled, "boo…."

Holly screamed and slid in the dirt, almost falling. "Oh, my God, you scared the shit out of me."

I laughed as Holly pushed me away from her.

* * *

The next day on our way to the Grand Canyon, we stopped at Lake Powell again and swam and cliff jumped for a couple of hours. From there, we drove to where the Horseshoe Bend was. Then we hiked back to a lookout where the bluish-green water of the Colorado river u-turned around a massive peaked red rock formation sitting in the riverbed.

"See the exit sign? It says we take I-40 to Las Vegas." Holly pointed.

"Vegas is not on our schedule, Holly." *Or is it and she didn't tell me?*

Holly smiled. "Well, we could take a detour, couldn't we?"

Oh, my God, what is Holly's fascination with going to Vegas? "We're not even old enough to gamble or drink legally, so why bother going there?"

"We'll talk about Vegas later."

"Yep, we'll talk about it later." I turned and watched the scenery come and go in slow motion flashes. *Maybe we should go if she really wants to—this is Holly's vacation too.*

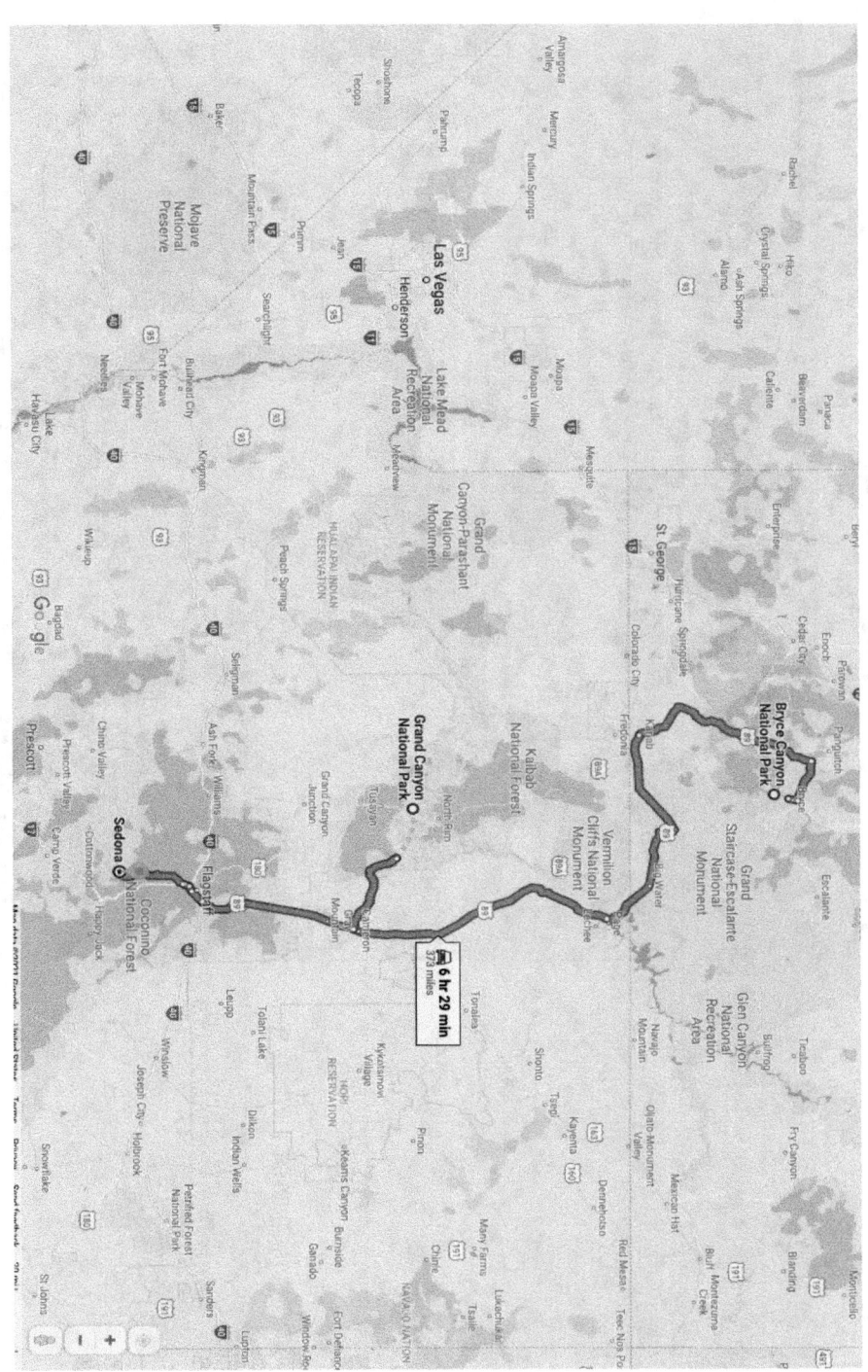

45

SEVEN

Just Because You Lose a Leg Doesn't Mean You Die

"Welcome to the South Rim of the Grand Canyon, an immense canyon where layers of greens and browns crisscross brilliant shades of red rock, and oranges and pinks dancing in the vivid sunlight cascading on the walls into the deep canyon. Camping is ten dollars per night, fifty percent off for seniors." We pulled up to the entrance of the park.

"Do you think if we tell them we're seniors, we'll get a discount?" I asked.

"They mean senior citizens. Not high school seniors, silly."

I shrugged my shoulder. "It's worth a try."

We paid the full price for camping. The park ranger informed us that high school seniors did not count towards the senior's discount, but he gave us an 'A' for trying and handed us a park map through the car window.

After we found the campground and set up our tent, we walked over to the rim of the canyon.

"Hey, Holly, I read about a ranch down at the bottom called Phantom Ranch. Can you see it?"

Holly squinted her eyes as she searched below. "There's a ranch down there?"

"Yep. The Bright Angel Trailhead takes you down to the bottom, but then we'd have to walk back up. Or we could take a mule ride down."

"No way am I getting on one of those. What if they slip and fall or bite you?"

"Yeah, that sounds dangerous." I paged through my National Parks book. "The Colorado River runs through the canyon, and they have one, three, and five-day rafting trips on the river." Then, my eyes landed on the listed price. "Ugh, I groaned "Never mind, they cost too much."

Holly leaned over my shoulder to glance at what I was reading. "How much is too much?"

"The one day is one hundred and five per person. The three-day trip is, eww, twelve hundred, and the five day is two thousand." *I guess I should have saved more money so I could do some of this stuff. I hate not having any money.*

"Yep. Way too much. What else is there to do?"

I turned the page. "There's a Grand Canyon Skywalk."

"What's that?"

"It's a horseshoe shaped glass walkway with a glass floor that you can see 4,000 feet below." *Yikes.* "But that's twenty-six per person." *Oh darn.* "Oh, oh, and ziplining. Damn, that's eighty-nine."

"Cool. I'd totally do the glass Skywalk and ziplining if they were cheaper. Let's just hike. I want to save my money so we can do things in California," Holly confidently stated

Excitement rose inside. "Yeah, me too."

We walked along the Rim Trail and looked out and into the canyon from all angles. Looking down at the shear drop-offs at the edge made my heart stop. There were no railings to hold on to, and large signs posted along the way cautioned people to stand back and watch their step. Many people die every year at the canyon because they misjudge the terrain at the canyon's edge. It was a mile down to the bottom if you fell.

"Aren't you the brave one, getting so close to the edge." Holly laughed.

"Well, not really." I backed up and lay on my belly. Small rocks scraped the skin on my arms and legs as I crawled to the edge.

"What the heck are you doing, girl?"

"I want to see over the edge, but I don't want to fall. Hold my legs so I won't fall off."

Holly leaned over and held onto my ankles. "What do you see?"

"It's so far down there, but I think I can see the Colorado River, but just barely, though." I slid closer to the edge and could just make out the winding shape of the river deep in the canyon. A few feet below, there was a hat on the rock ledge. One minute that hat had been on someone's head, and then it was part of the scenery.

Holly crawled next to me and hooked her arm around mine. "I think we need to hang on to each other."

"This is ridiculous, how big the Grand Canyon is. It's a giant hole in the ground. I'm used to looking up at the mountains in Colorado."

"I know. The map says it's ten miles across and one mile down. Can you believe it?"

I got lost in the deep red, orange, and green layered landscape around me.

After thirty seconds of staring in wonder, Holly broke the silence. "You know people probably think we're crazy, don't you? Is that a hat down there?"

"Yep. And I don't care if anyone thinks I'm crazy, safety first." A few seconds later, a couple of people joined us on the ground, crawling up to the edge. We turned toward each other and smiled.

On our way back to the campground, we passed a mule barn where mules waited their turn to walk down to the Phantom Ranch at the bottom of the canyon on a narrow dirt trail with visitors on their backs. We held out our hands to pet them and wished them luck on their next ride down the canyon. Elk and deer wandered through the campground under the pine and spruce trees. Holly said, "let's change and go get something to eat." We crawled inside the tent and took off our shirts. I reached inside my backpack and grabbed my deodorant. Holly was dressed and unzipped the tent to leave. She stopped and backed away. Then she crept behind me.

"What are you doing?"

"Oh, my God, that's a huge spider," she quietly said.

My voice quivered. "What?"

She peeked around my shoulder. "No...no, wait, I think it's a tarantula."

"What...? Where?" I scooted backward—very slowly.

"There, there!" She pointed at the front of our tent.

A black hairy spider with brown fuzzy legs was creeping in the pine needles and dried leaves right at the edge of our tent. I tried backing up to get behind Holly, but our arms tangled. "What should we do?"

"Kill it!," she shrieked.

I pushed her shoulder. "No, you kill it."

"Just step on it."

My eyes never left the spider. "With what? I'm on my knees."

"We can't let this spider get inside our tent."

"I know. Hand me my shoe." My heart pounded. "Holly?...Can spiders jump?"

"Spiders don't jump...I don't think. Just step on it."

I inched my way to the edge with my favorite pair of tennis shoes. "Holly? What if it bites me? Will I die?"

"I don't think so, but maybe if you're allergic to it."

My throat tightened. "How do you know if you are allergic to spiders?"

"I don't know. I guess you'll find out if it bites you."

I turned and glared at Holly. "That's not what I want to hear, Holly." I slid closer to Harry the tarantula. He didn't move. "Maybe he's already dead."

"No, he's not dead. He's still moving...see?"

"How can you see anything when you're behind me?"

"I can see perfectly. He's alive." Holly slid next to me and pointed. "There he goes. Get him!"

Harry started scuttling in my direction. Holly scrambled behind me again. I sat up on my knees and smashed my shoe down on top of him.

"Where is he? Did you get him? Is he dead?"

"He's under my shoe." I think. I lifted my shoe gently and backed away. "I think I got him."

"What do you mean you think? Is he dead or not? Please tell me he's dead," she whined.

I leaned in closer. "Ah, no, I think he just lost a leg." My voice quivered. "He's still moving,"

"Damn it. How can he be moving when he's missing a leg?"

"Because he's got seven more?" I slid back by Holly. "I need to think about this. Um…I snapped my fingers behind me. "Hand me my other shoe."

Holly scrabbled to find my other shoe. "Maybe if you smash his other legs, they'll fall off, and then he'll finally die, or at least not be able to get to us."

I took a deep breath and rested my hand over my stomach. "All right. I'm going in." Harry was still moving. I raised both arms above my head and crushed the spider, first with one shoe and then the other. It squished beneath my shoes. "I think he's dead now." I scrapped him off the bottom of my shoe, buried him under the leaves outside our tent, and then fell back on my sleeping bag. *I just killed a spider, a giant spider. Yep, I'm powerful and strong. Eek, but it was a little scary and creepy at the same time. But I killed a spider, a dark, ugly, scary spider.*

Later in the day, we stopped at the edge of the canyon after doing laundry and showering on the way back to the campground. The evening shadows of the sun setting climbed the red walls slowly, transforming the canyon into mass blackness until the moon rose high and spotlighted the canyon.

Back at the campground, our fire pit was empty. I looked in the direction of burning wood. Our tent neighbors had a nice roaring fire going in their fire pit. "Hey, Holly, let's go ask where they got their wood from."

She walked over to me. "We don't know them. What if they're weirdos?"

I rolled my eyes. "Holly, it's an old man and woman. I think we'll be okay."

"Okay, but if they turn out to be weirdos, don't tell me I didn't warn you."

We walked over but kept our distance, in case Holly was right.

I waived to an older man wearing a ball cap and glasses. "Hi, um, do you know where we can get some wood to build a fire?"

The man shook his head. "Ich verstehe kein Englisch."

I looked over at Holly. "Ah...?"

A younger man with long blond hair crawled out of the tent next to them. "Was wollen sie?"

The older man pointed toward us.

"Englisch?"

I nodded and pointed at their fire pit. "Ah, yeah, we were wondering where to get wood for the fire."

"Du buy wood from Laden...store." He pointed across the campground.

"Okay, thanks." I turned to leave.

"Du can...how du say, hangen.... He pointed at their campsite. "Hier...here."

I looked over at Holly. "What do you think? We won't have to buy wood."

Holly shrugged her shoulders. "I guess." She paused. "Okay. Let's do it because I don't know how to start a fire anyway or have matches."

We stepped closer to their circle.

"Mein name Heinrich." He pointed around their campsite. "This mein Vater, um, Father, and Mutter, and Bruder Alfred." Alfred opened two folding chairs. "Bitte setzen."

I pointed to myself. "I'm Sandy." Then, I pointed at Holly. "And this is Holly."

Heinrich pointed at the chairs. "Er says bitte…please setz."

"Where are you guys from?" I asked slowly.

Heinrich and his brother laughed. "Wir sind aus Germany," Alfred said.

Holly's eyes widened with curiosity. "Wow, that's pretty cool that you guys came all the way here from Germany."

"The United States is…Schon…How du sagen…say beauty…."

"Beautiful," I said. *Yes, our country is beautiful.*

"Ja." The father smiled, nodding his head.

"Would you like a selter?" Heinrich asked. He lifted a soda can.

Holly and I both nodded. "Yeah, thanks. Sorry, we don't speak German."

Heinrich smiled. "Es ist okay."

We sat around the crackling fire for an hour, talking in English while our German friends spoke in German and English. "We learn from you when you speak," Heinrich said.

We told them about our spider adventure and how I killed it. Our German friends had a good laugh at our story about Harry. It was easy to talk to Heinrich and Alfred, even with their limited English. And they translated everything we said to their mother and father. They nodded their heads as if they understood. We all managed to try to understand each other. It was our first foreign language lesson learning with our new friends. Just like Heinrich said, they learn from us when we speak.

A bright flashing light flickered on and off through our tent woke me up. My heart jumped. I nudged Holly and whispered. "Holly. I think someone's outside."

"What?" Holly mumbled.

"Shhhhh, see the light?"

Holly yawned. "No. I don't see any lig...."

I scrambled out of my sleeping bag. "There it is again."

"What do you think it is?"

Light flickered through our tent again.

I slid to the back of the tent. "Do you think it's a bear?"

"I don't think bears carry flashlights," Holly whispered brushing up next to me. "Go check it out."

"Why me?"

"You said you need to be braver."

"When did I say that?"

"I don't remember, but now would be a good time for you to be brave."

I inched my way on the ground to the opening, slowly unzipped the flap, and propped myself on my elbows. I looked around for where the light could be coming from. I was silent. "I don't see anyth—" A clap of thunder exploded above. We both screamed. I pushed back inside, crawling under my sleeping bag. "Oh, my God, that scared me." The tent lit up again.

We poked our heads out of the tent.

"Is it raining?" I asked turning my head toward the sky waiting to be hit with drops of cold rain.

Holly held out her hand. "I don't feel anything. It looks like it's a lightning storm."

Further away, bright sparks of jagged electricity clawed across the black sky. Thunder rolled, cracked, and boomed in the darkness, and then flashing lights spider-webbed from high above down to the earth. We watched for a few minutes and then crawled back inside the tent and fell back asleep to nature's night light.

Shortly after sunrise and breakfast, we hiked the South Kaibab Trail. It took us most of the day. Along the way, many more visitors shouted out to each other, sometimes laughing, sometimes scolding, sometimes in English, sometimes in one of a dozen other languages. So many people took in the majestic Grand Canyon. Even though we didn't understand what was said, we all understood beauty when we saw it. It was universal, regardless of language.

The next day, we took the tent down and packed the car. Holly drove over to the Bright Angel Lodge, where we bought ice cream and walked to the edge of the rim. We gazed out across the canyon in silence, taking in one last look before we said goodbye to nature's beautiful canyon.

Holly nudged my arm. "Do you remember in the movie *Thelma and Louise?* This is where they drove off the cliff in the Grand Canyon when the cops chasing them."

"Oh yeah, this is it." I continued to stare out across the canyon. "Let's not do that." *Let's not drive off a cliff to end this story.*

EIGHT

We Became Cactus Girls

"The spiritual meaning behind the cactus is symbolized in its hard protective exterior, endurance, and strength to survive in new environments and situations. The pale-green cactus, protected by many thorns, grows in the hot desert sun where no other plants could grow and requires very little water. As a result, they can retain all the water they get. A couple of times a year, they bloom with beautiful flowers."

I unfolded the brochure for Sedona. "Welcome to Sedona, Arizona. The Spiritual Red Rock Country."

"This brochure doesn't tell me much." I pulled my book out of my backpack and flipped to Sedona. "Okay, here's some things to do." I read through the pages. A Red Rock balloon ride. Two hundred twenty-five, per person. *Sounds fun but scary and expensive.* Next. Pink Jeep Tours. Off-road in a pink Jeep to famous rocks and sites. One hundred twenty-four, per person. *Too much. Besides, pink is not my favorite color.* I closed the book and tossed it in the back seat. "Um, there's some cool stuff to do, but everything is so expensive. I think we should do things on our own and save our money. We can check out some of the rock formations. There's Cathedral Rock and Bell Rock, which are the most famous. They should

57

be coming up on the left. It also says there are vortexes there. And the best part is we don't have to pay for anything."

We parked and hiked along the red dirt trail, scanning the red-rock landscape around us to Cathedral Rock. Clumps of purplish prickly pear cactus dotted the red desert. Off in the distance, tall green, spiny Saguaro cactuses with three, four, or five branches resembling thorny arms sticking up in the air decorated the desert. Along the trail, brown long-eared jackrabbits and brownish-red lizards blended with the Sedona dirt. They hopped and scattered around the sagebrush and over the broken red rocks bordering the pathway. You can tell the difference between a regular rabbit and a jackrabbit. Jackrabbits have long ears that stick straight up and long back legs.

Holly stopped. "Okay, I give up. What is a vortex?"

"The book says something about energy and healing stuff. And that many people feel inspired, recharged, or uplifted after visiting a vortex."

When we arrived at Cathedral Rock, many women were meditating and stretching in yoga poses. We stood and watched for a moment.

"Ask them if they know where the vortexes are."

"Maybe we should wait until they're done."

A couple of women walked by me dressed in yoga pants and tie-dyed bandanas wrapped around their gray hair. "Excuse me?"

The women turned.

She wore no makeup. I could see deep into her calm light blue eyes. "We read there's vortexes here. Can you show us where they are?"

"Oh, sweetie, vortexes are spirits traveling freely between our world and the other side."

Yikes. Is that a good thing or a bad thing?

She rested her hand over her heart. "Vortexes are anywhere you feel them."

Holly stepped forward. "How will we know if it's a vortex?"

"Well, you'll feel a range of sensations." She closed her eyes. "When you encounter a vortex, you'll either feel a slight tingling or a flutter of some sort." She opened her eyes. "Some people feel a vibration across the nape of their neck and the shoulder blades." She pointed at the others meditating. "First, you need to find a spot that feels right and rest your mind, your body, and soul. Then, let the uplifting spiritual power take you away."

"Then what?" I asked.

She placed her hand on my chest. "Go to the place inside yourself and let the energy of the earth heal you, or you can do some self-exploration if that's what the energy is calling you to do."

A knot rested in the back of my throat.

"Take a walk around. And when you feel it… you'll know. The vortex energy provides wings so you can fly."

Holly and I looked at each other after the women walked away.

"It sounds kinda spooky in a way," Holly said.

"I guess. But I want to try it. What can it hurt?"

Holly giggled. "My, my, what a brave girl you are."

"Ha-ha. Very funny."

We sat off to the side of the rock so we wouldn't disturb anyone. I mimicked one woman sitting cross legged with her hands in a prayer pose in front of her heart. When she breathed in deeply, I breathed deeply. When she pulled her shoulders back and let out a breath, I pulled my shoulders back and exhaled. But I felt nothing. I closed my eyes, but the sounds of wings flapping and birds screeching above broke my concentration.

I opened one eye and leaned into Holly, and whispered. "I'm not feeling anything, are you?"

Holly whispered back. "No. Maybe this isn't the right spot."

"Do you think everyone here is faking it?"

"I don't know, but what I do know is I'm hungry. So, pass the cheese crackers."

After a few minutes of hiking and looking out at the rock formations surrounding us, and trying to find a vortex, we walked back to the car. We drove to another famous vortex spot, Bell Rock. We followed the Bell Rock loop toward the Bell Plateau. Our shadows skipped along on the side of the trail, skimming over rocks, through sagebrush bushes, and around the spiny cactuses.

When we reached the plateau, we found an area among some flat rocks. I propped my backpack behind my head and leaned back.

Holly passed me the crackers. "Want some?"

I reached for them.

"It looks like you have a friend." She pointed next to me.

A brown-feathered roadrunner patiently waited for a cracker. I reached my hand out. "Want a cracker?" He hopped a little closer, his ruffled head a tad lower. "Come get it." His head bobbed, then he leaned back, showing his white underbelly. I tossed a piece of cracker near him. He darted over, grabbed it, and dashed off.

After eating a few more crackers, I brushed my hands off, leaned back on my elbows, and stared up at the cloudless blue sky. The warmth of the afternoon sun bathed my body, and the sky disappeared behind the backs of my eyelids. My body softened in the heat of the red earth, and I dreamed.

An ocean wave of water rushed over me. I stared, but I couldn't see. Deep in the rippling water was a younger me. A pixie haircut, wearing a blue and white striped sailor dress. A smile that wasn't there. A slow frown formed on my face as I watched a younger me. My trembling arms opened to draw her in. I whispered, "Everything will be okay. I will protect you." But how could I? I was afraid for her—I knew her life. My body tightened as another wave rolled in. I had long hair and braces. I was wearing my older sister's favorite shirt, the one she told me never ever to touch. It hung low and fell off my shoulders. A tightness rose in my chest, I lowered my head. But I still loved the yellow and brown knit smock top.

Why was I seeing this? What did this mean? The scents of cedar, sandalwood, and amber incense swirled in the air, mixing with joy and happiness surrounding me. My friends were there, and my favorite songs played on the stereo in the background. Holly was there too, just as she was with me that day. A smile, deep down inside, waited to come. Waves rushed around me. I reached in the water to catch it. The wave rose high above, lifting me. My mother appeared, but she was deep in the ocean. I reached out to her, but my hands were tied and restrained. She drifted further away. I tried to swim to her, but I couldn't move. I looked down at my arms and legs. Now, they were both tied down, and then she was gone.

"Hey, hey." Holly tapped on my shoulder, kneeling over me.

My eyes sprang open. "What, what?"

"Did you feel anything?"

I sat up and stopped a tear from rolling down my cheek. "I…I think I did. Did you?"

"Yeah, I kinda had a weird feeling, like a really cool vibe, like I was somewhere else—far away."

"Did you see anything, and what did you see?"

"There was bright flashing neon lights, bells dinging all around me. I don't know where I was, but everyone was happy, and I was happy."

Yeah, I was happy too…. "I think we should go."

Holly agreed. I brushed the red dirt off my shorts and backpack, and Holly and I started back down the trail. I hesitated and turned around. Holly kept walking. I looked back at Bell Rock. *Did I just get my wings?*

I caught up with Holly. "So, tell me, what did you feel?" she asked.

"It was weird. I was so relaxed. And then I saw my life in ocean waves. I know it doesn't make sense. Waves washed up on the shore, and then I was carried away out to sea…." I rested my hand on my chest. "I don't know. Maybe I fell asleep or something, but I feel pretty good, like everything is past me, like… I'm…enough."

Holly wrapped her arms around me. "You are enough. And don't you forget it."

A smile sank deep inside. "Thanks, Holly."

Further down the trail, a brown long-eared jackrabbit hurried toward us. I turned and watched him scurry up the trail. *I wonder where he's going so fast.* Large, dark birds circled overhead, cawing. Smaller birds scattered. *What's going on?* I turned back to the trail. "Oh my God!"

"What?" Holly asked from behind me.

I motioned for Holly to stop and whispered. "Um, Holly…." I pointed down the trail. "I think that's a snake."

We slowly stepped back. My body stiffened. "What do we do?" My heart raced. "He's right in the middle of the path."

Holly grabbed my shoulder, digging her nails into me. Um, um, I think snakes are supposed to be more afraid of us, right?"

"Are you asking or telling me?"

"I don't know, but I'm not afraid of snakes," Holly said, backing up. "Um, find a stick. Maybe we can shoo him away?"

"Why me? I thought you weren't afraid of snakes?"

"I'm not, but…."

"Then why are you backing away, girlfriend?"

"Ah, to give you more room. Um, you're the brave one now. And you said you need to stop being afraid of everything, didn't you?"

She took another step back.

Whatever. I looked around along the path. *Okay, I can do this—I think. I need to find something…* nothing but sagebrush bushes and a few rocks. I slowly bent down. I kept my eyes on the snake and grabbed the nearest rock. *Wait, maybe this is a geode.* I shook the rock and then held it up in the sunlight to make sure it wasn't a geode. I didn't want to have dead snake parts on my geode if it really was one. I glanced back and forth at the rock and then at the snake to make sure he wasn't getting too close.

The brown spotted snake sidewinded toward us. *Oh shit.* Holly and I grabbed each other and jerked back. "No, no, bad snake! Sit. Stay." When we jumped back again, our feet tangled, and we tripped over the edge of the trail. Dirt and stones kicked up underneath our feet when we fell.

"What the hell…?" I yelled. I lifted my hand. Prickly needles were sticking out of my hands, arms, and legs.

"Oh, my God, I think we just landed on a cactus," Holly yelled out.

I raised my hands. I had thorns and needles all over me. "Holly, are you covered in thorns too?"

Holly lifted her arms. "Yep. I have these damned things everywhere."

I couldn't get up. Thorns and tiny needles were everywhere on my body. "Holly, what happened to the snake?" Holly and I scanned the trail around us. Oh, *please be gone.*

"I...I don't see him anymore. I think he's gone," Holly said.

Thank God. I pulled a large needle from my leg. It left a little blood spot. "I can't believe we fell into a stupid cactus."

"Are you two girls okay?"

My heart jumped. We looked up at two guys standing over us, blocking the sunlight. They squatted near us.

I couldn't back away because of the needles in my hands. "I think so. I guess we fell into a cactus."

"I can see that. It looks like you fell into a Cholla Cactus."

I glanced over. "What is a Cholla Cactus?"

He pointed next to me and Holly. "That's a Cholla Cactus. See how it has long spiny stems that look like arms?"

"How did you girls fall?" The tall one asked.

"There was a snake, and...and...he charged at us, then we tripped and fell." I pointed down the path. "You don't see the snake, do you?"

"No, I don't see the snake. You probably scared it off when you fell."

I looked over at Holly, trying to pick the needles out of her hands and legs. I raised my hands. "Do you know how we get these little stickers out?"

"These damned things hurt. I can't even grab them to get them out," Holly yelled.

"By the way, I'm Steve, and this is Ron. Do either of you have duct tape?" The man asked.

Duct tape? My dad has like 40 rolls of duct tape at home. But I don't live with him anymore, so it doesn't matter anyway. I wonder if Dan had duct tape? Why didn't he tell me to bring duct tape?

Holly and I shook our heads. "Ah, no, we don't."

"Okay, how about tweezers?"

Holly grabbed her backpack. "Yeah, I have tweezers." She tried to unzip a side pocket, but she couldn't because of the stickers.

Ron held out his hand. "Here, let me help you." He unzipped the pocket, reached inside, and pulled out her sunscreen, lip gloss, and tweezers.

"You're going to have to pull each one out. One at a time." Ron pinched Holly's skin and grabbed a tiny needle with the tweezers. "They're tricky. So, try and get as many of them out as possible. You'll probably keep finding them for a few days."

Steve and Ron helped us up. "You girls going to be okay?"

"Yeah, um, I think we'll be okay. Thanks for helping us," I said.

"Yeah, thanks," Holly said.

"No problem," Steve said. "Be careful out there now. Nature is beautiful, but it can be dangerous too."

Yeah, I think I just figured that out. Spiders, snakes, and cactus.

Ron and Steve took off down the path.

Holly handed me the tweezers. I pulled a few stickers out of my hand. "What if we were like a cactus and had needles and thorns all over us? Nobody would mess with us."

Holly raised her thorny hands. "Stay away from me, or I'll hurt you."

I laughed. "Yeah!" *I could protect myself from everyone who tried to hurt me.*

"Yep, we could be the Cactus Girls."

"Cactus Girls!" We both said and high-fived each other.

"Ouch, ouch, ouch."

We walked back to the car and spent the next hour removing the needles from all over our bodies.

ψ ψ ψ

The next day, we drove out to Slide Rock State Park in Oak Creek Canyon, just fifteen minutes from Sedona, with a natural rock water slide located inside the park. Green Cypress and Juniper trees decorated Slide Rock, contrasting with the red-rock landscape.

We changed into our bathing suits in the car and climbed up to the top of Slide Rock. We waited behind many other tourists to slide down the chilled rock water slide from Oak Creek that rushed over the algae-coated slide rock. The slick water carried us down through rippling and splashing water into a cold pool of calm at the end of the slide. After a few more turns, we waded in the water and then dangled our feet over the edge of the sunbaked rock, listening to the kids laughing and watching them jumping and splattering the cool water over themselves.

"Although the vortex was pretty cool, I'm still bummed that we haven't found any geodes."

Holly reached over the edge into the rushing water and pulled a handful of small colorful river rocks out. She picked through the pile and placed a shiny red rock in my hand. "I know it's not a geode, but it is shiny and pretty."

I rubbed the rock between my fingers and then glanced over at Holly basking in the sun. "I can still feel the sharp spines in my hands from our cactus encounter yesterday."

"Me too." Holly laughed.

"What's so funny?" I asked.

"I was just thinking about the tarantula, and the snake, and everything. You were pretty brave."

"Well, not really. One of us had to do something." I nudged her shoulder.

"You weren't afraid to kill the spider or when the snake was blocking our way."

"Oh, I was afraid of the snake."

"So, what else are you afraid of?"

I thought for a minute. "I guess I'd have to say…men, men scare me the most."

Holly rolled toward me. "What do you mean? You weren't afraid of Steven and Ron?"

"I don't know. I guess maybe because I don't understand them? Guys don't always tell you the truth, and every time I get involved with some guy, I end up getting hurt. And Steve and Ron were there to help, not hurt."

She rolled back over and looked up in the sky. "I hear ya."

I turned and leaned on my side. "What are you afraid of?"

"I'm afraid of spiders," Holly said.

"Really?" I laughed. "You afraid of spiders? I guess I'm afraid of big hairy spiders."

Holly giggled. "I'm afraid of flying too."

"Why flying? It's supposed to be safer than driving."

"I think it's a control thing."

"So, you're afraid of not having control," I said.

"Exactly."

"A few months ago, I learned from Dan to just say fuck it. But, having control isn't easy."

"True. You just gotta roll with it, right, girl?"

"Yep. This is good. I'm glad we had a breakthrough. You're such a good shrink."

We both laughed.

"I'm ready to move on to San Diego tomorrow."

"Yep, I am too," Holly said.

"No more spiders, snakes…."

"Wild coyotes…."

"Cliffs to fall from…."

"And cacti."

I sat up quickly. "Ugh. Yes, those damned cacti."

"We survived. That's all that matters."

I leaned back on the rock. A smile crossed my lips. *Yeah, we are the Cactus Girls.*

"Hey, Karen, it's me. Sorry I haven't called in a while. We've been busy. First, we went to Bryce Canyon. The hoodoos were kinda cool and mysterious. I swear I could hear them talking. But it's incredible how water and wind erosion can cut through and shape the mountains and rock. Then we made it to the Grand Canyon. It was a massive, awe-inspiring hole in the ground. So amazing, though. We hiked along the rim, but not too close, though, if you fell, you'd be a goner. We met a friendly German family at the campground. They invited Holly and me to hang out at their campfire. It was fun trying to talk to each other because they didn't know much English, except for the two boys, who both spoke some English. Oh, and then a huge tarantula spider tried to get into our tent. It was as big as my hand." I held my hand up. "Well, maybe not as big as my hand, but it was huge. And then it charged toward us. I thought we were goners, so I smashed it with my shoe and killed it. It's not against the law to kill a spider, is it? It was either him or us.

We went to Slide Rock Park and slid down the rock slide. That was so cool too, and now we are leaving Sedona. It's so pretty up here with the red rock. We took several hikes and found a vortex. Do you know what a vortex is? It was cool in a weird way. I'm not sure I know what to think about it. It made me feel alive—refreshed. Kinda like I'm a different person now.

Oh, and on the way down the trail, a brown-and-white speckled snake was waiting for us on the side of the trail—I think it was a massive cobra. Do they have cobras in Arizona? Anyway, it probably could have eaten us alive. I was going to kill it with a rock, but then it came at us, and we tripped and fell into a cactus. We had thorns and sharp spines everywhere. It hurt so much. And then some nice guys showed us how to get the stickers out with tweezers. Dan should have told me to bring duct tape. And now Holly and I are calling ourselves "Cactus Girls." Everything is so expensive, but we're saving our money for California, and I still haven't found any geodes. Anyway, thanks again for the National Parks pass. It really helped to get into the parks for free. Well, I'm signing off now. We are off to San Diego. I gotta get going. Talk to you later."

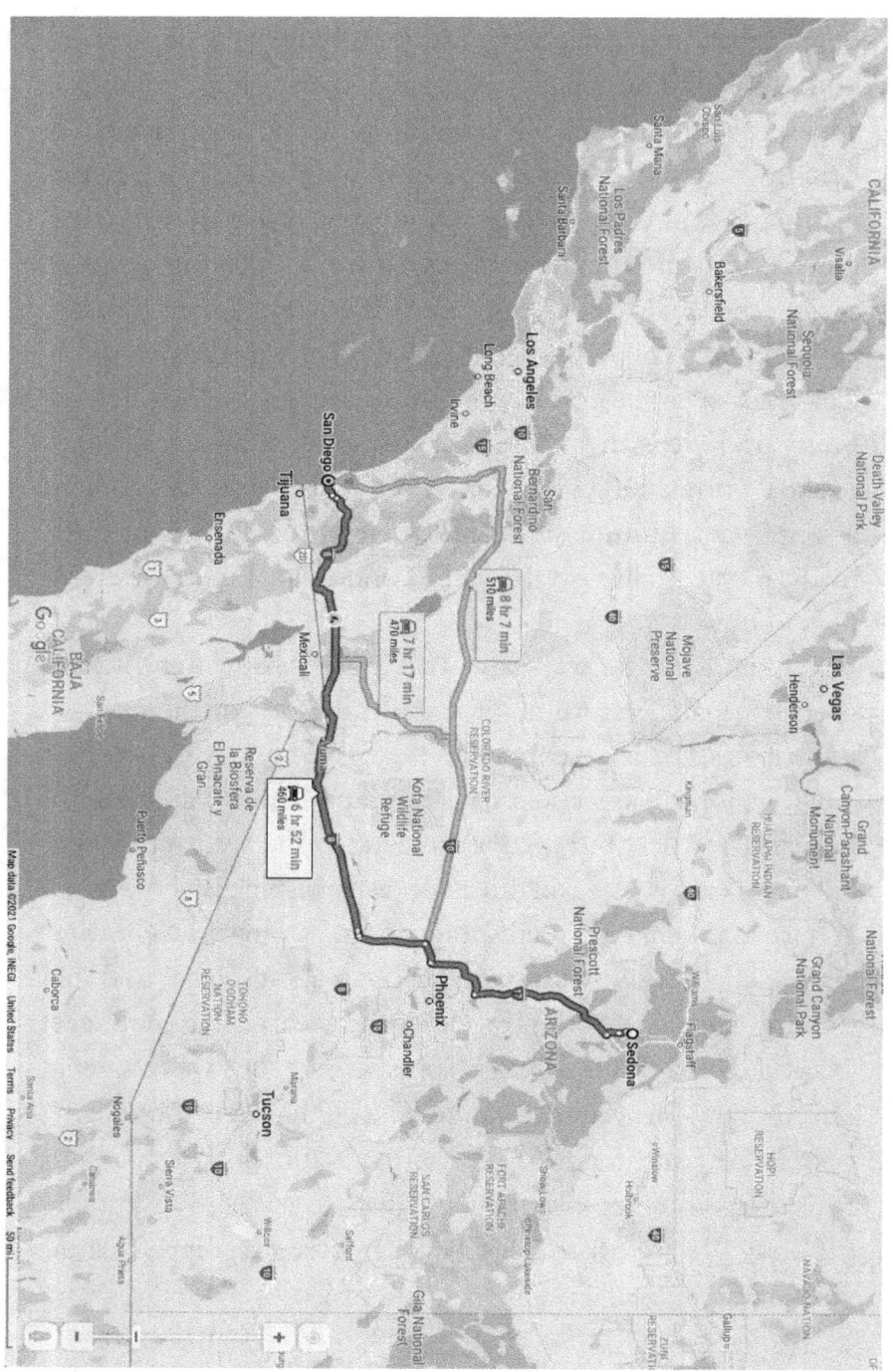

NINE

Take Me Away — Desert Highway

In the morning, we started our six-hour journey to San Diego, California. Wind turbine farms littered the vacant land, and wildflowers bloomed along both sides of the desert highway. The road cut through Indian Reservations, where every small single-story house and trailer either had boards on the windows or no windows at all, and some had curtains flapping in and out of open windows. Old trucks and campers with cracked windshields and missing one or more tires cluttered their unfenced yards. Clotheslines sagged with torn blankets, sheets, and jeans. A mile down the road, a single wide trailer hitched up against a dead tree, half its windows covered in boards. I thought it was abandoned at first. Then, the door opened, and a gray-haired old man eased himself down the rickety front steps. As I turned in my seat, I watched him open the door of a beat-up Chevy truck. A lump rose in my throat. I wondered if he had once ridden his pony across the desert, nothing on but a smile and the wind in his hair.

It was sad to see Native Americans who once occupied and founded our beautiful land living so poorly. I couldn't imagine that this was their choice.

The following highway exit sign advertised the Golden Acorn Casino, and further down was a small wooden arrow sign pointing down a dirt road for the Coyote's Flying Saucer Repair shop. I wondered if aliens ever brought their flying saucers in for repairs.

We stopped for fresh fruit and avocados at a fruit stand off the highway. On a small table next to the counter were handmade braided and beaded Indian bracelets. Holly picked out a purple, blue, and green bracelet, and I found a red, orange, and yellow one. We tied them around each other's wrists. I handed the woman a five-dollar bill. "I love these. They're so pretty."

The Indian woman nodded.

"Hey, that was a pretty cool-looking lizard running across the road when we pulled up," Holly said.

"Oh, those aren't lizards. Those are Gila monsters."

My eyebrows lifted in surprise. *A Gila monster? Are they for real? Wasn't there a movie with a giant Gila monster in it? I thought those were only make-believe monsters in the movies.*

"Jes, Gila's bigger. Black with orange and pink, they very poisonous, so be careful walking round. Don't try to pet em."

Um, you can bet I won't be petting any Gila monsters.

I stepped lightly walking back to the car. *Holly better not expect me to kill a Gila monster if we see one. It's her turn. I'm done killing things.*

Saguaro cactus backdropped the Sonora desert. Juniper forests and gnarled trees appeared and then disappeared. The landscape changed along the way, becoming more desolate as we traveled on.

"Okay, Holly, if you could be any kind of animal, what would it be and why?"

She thought for a minute. "I guess I would want to be a tiger because I love cats. Tigers are strong, powerful, and independent. And I love black and orange. How about you?"

I pictured the wild horses running free on our way out here. "Well, I would want to be a wild horse. They're friendly, generous, independent, and free-spirited. So beautiful and talented. And they can run fast to escape predators. And they can be wild and free."

"Not all horses are wild and free. What if you're a horse living on a farm?"

"Well, then I'd hope I had a nice family to take care of me with lots of room to run and roam." *I want to be free and run like horses do, but not run away. I want to be where I can be happy and free, but is there such a place?*

TEN

Letting Go of Everything I've Learned from You

"Welcome to San Diego. Known for its miles of white sandy beaches, perfect weather, sand, sun, and fun."

We crossed the state line into California. "Okay, where are we going first?" Holly asked.

"The beach!" we both shouted.

I opened the California book and paged to San Diego. "There's Ocean Beach, Mission Beach, Pacific Beach, Imperial Beach."

"Which one is closest?"

"Imperial Beach is by the Mexican border."

"Nope. Next."

"Then there's Ocean Beach."

Ocean Beach was a massive surf mecca. Surfers, kiteboarders, and paddleboarders fought for their space in the water and waves. It was like gang turfs in the streets.

Sand squished between our toes as we waded out into the waves. The salty ocean air surrounded our bodies as the white-capped waves splashed up to our stomachs. Holly dove in first, and then I followed.

We watched surfers riding the waves for a few minutes and then swam near them. We asked if they would show us how to surf. They all answered the same way. "NO! Go back where you came from."

I shrugged my shoulders. "What's wrong with them?"

A couple of girls next to us laughed. "Surfers are very territorial. They don't like it when you breathe their air and are in their space."

"So, they think they own the beach and water?"

"Yep. You don't mess with surfers at Ocean Beach. Try Mission Beach. It's only a few miles up the coast. The surfers are friendlier there."

Twenty minutes later, we were walking along the boardwalk on Mission Beach. The aroma of spicy Buffalo wings and grilled hamburgers and onions made my stomach rumble as we walked by restaurant after restaurant.

"I'm hungry for real food," I said.

"Me too. No more sandwiches and cheese crackers."

"Want to split a burger and fries?"

"You're on, but I want cheese fries."

We ordered at the takeout window and sat on the concrete wall along the boardwalk to eat. Bike riders and skateboarders weaved in and around people. *I'd end up in the hospital if I tried skateboarding.* People were playing volleyball in the sand. Seagulls swooped down, trying to snatch a cheese fry when we weren't looking.

After eating, we stretched out on our beach towels and watched the waves roll up on the shore, spreading across the sand. Surfers waiting to catch a wave bobbed up and down on their boards in the white-capped water.

"Holly, we need to try surfing."

"I know, but where are we going to get a surfboard?"

"I'm sure there's a place around here. Let's go in the water and then look for one later."

We passed a cute lifeguard walking the beach on the way to the water and stared at him for longer than we should have. In our defense, he had a lot to look at, but I couldn't tell you what color his shorts were. *Maybe I should pretend to drown myself in the ocean so he'll come to save me.*

Holly and I counted to three, and we ran into the water, splashing and kicking up sand and water behind us until we dove under the waves. The cold Pacific water was refreshing, but it took a while to get used to it. Along the shore, young kids were building sandcastles using paper cups. They dug trenches around their castles with their hands to keep their make-believe enemies out. When they poured water from their cups into the trench, their castles washed away. Further back, little ones giggled as they tossed one last pile of sand onto their older siblings buried in the sand up to their necks while older kids on bodyboards sailed across small waves breaking near the shore.

"Hey, Holly, that looks like something we could do. Let's go see if we can find one of those boards."

We dried off and walked along the boardwalk, passing trinket and souvenir shops selling tank tops and tee shirts with peace signs, pot leaves, and rainbows with unicorns. Crowded outdoor restaurants either played the Mamas and the Papas 'California Dreamin' or the reggae vibes of Bob Marley. This was California. Oh, my God, *I love it here. I think I could stay here forever.*

Across the street, we found a surf shop and rented two bodyboards for the day. The owner made sure we had the right size board and demonstrated how to paddle and kick with our hips at the end of the board. Walking back, the scent of marijuana hung in the air after skateboarders and joggers passed by us. Smoking pot was illegal, but nobody seemed to care, and it became a familiar smell that came and went the rest of the day.

Back on the beach, Holly and I managed to ride a few waves to the shore on our bodyboards, but later we just floated on them. The waves tossed us back and forth and eventually tipped us over on the beach. Waves washed over us, leaving sand in our swimsuit bottoms.

Before dinner, we returned our boards and walked along the boardwalk, looking for something cheap but good to eat. Rapid-speaking Mexicans were selling tacos from trucks on every corner, so we decided to give the authentic California street tacos a try. I chose the tender shredded pork on the small round corn tortilla. The onions crunched when I took a bite. Bright-green slightly spiced cilantro leaves and fresh Verde sauce fulfilled my wishful expectations.

After sundown, we bought shaved ices and strolled along the beach. The only sound was the ocean waves rushing and crashing on the shore. Lights from boats out on the water twinkled on and off as they sailed by. It was the smoky smell of wood burning in the fire pits and music and laughter on the beach that caught our attention.

"Hey, ladies, care to join us?" A man dressed in jeans, a dark hoodie, and wearing a red bandana tied around his head yelled in our direction.

We shuffled barefoot in the sand over to them. The fire crackled, and yellow flames rose as they lapped the night air. The familiar aroma of marijuana hung in the air.

"Have a seat." He pointed around the group. "This is Rachel, Christian, Sasha. I'm Russell, and the man with the guitar is the one and only Poetry Man." The glow from the fire lit up everyone's faces. They were older than Holly and Me. The Poetry Man, sitting cross-legged in the sand, lifted his head, catching the moonlight reflecting in his wire-rimmed glasses while strumming his guitar.

Sasha and Christian wore sunglasses even though it was night. They slid over, making room for us. Sasha's long, dark dreadlocks swayed as she moved. *Her dreads are so cool.* We sat cross-legged in the sand. "Hey, everyone. I'm Sandy."

"And I'm Holly."

The Poetry Man strummed his guitar. "Sandy and Holly, come join us, come join us, tell us your story. I just want you to know we are not dangerous or predatory. I am the Poetry Man...I make everything all right."

The group laughed. "You'll have to forgive the Poetry Man. Ah, this is his vibe. He rhymes instead of speaking," Russell said.

"Well, not everything rhymes all the time," Rachel jumped in.

"Oh, Rachel, oh, Rachel, you just don't understand. I am a poet, not a singer in a band. I am the Poetry Man...I make everything all right."

Oh my God, this guy is crazy, well, kind of funny too.

"So, where are you girls from?" Christian asked.

"We're from Chicago, um, I'm from Chicago. Sandy was until she moved to Breckenridge, Colorado last year," Holly said.

The guitar strummed. "Chicago, Chicago the concrete jungle, when the wind blows in, then you're in trouble. It's known for being windy, but not because of the weather. It's the politicians who can't work together. I'm the Poetry Man...I make everything all right."

"Are all you guys from San Diego?" I asked.

"We all are now," Russell said.

Christian and Sasha nodded.

How cool would it be to live in San Diego and be able to go to the beach every day? What kind of a job could I get here so I could stay?

Russell opened a cooler next to him. "Can I get you something to drink?"

"Ah, no, we're good." I lifted my shaved ice. "We have these."

The guitar strummed. "Shaved ice, shaved ice, isn't that nice. I am the Poetry Man...I make everything all right."

"So, how long have you girls been in San Diego, and what have you been doing?" Sasha asked.

"We got here today."

Holly jumped in. "We went to the beach and boogie boarded."

"And had street tacos. That's all so far."

"We were thinking of going to Sea World tomorrow."

The guitar started. "Sea World, Sea World, take all of our money, there's sea life in the ocean, life on the sand, life all around you, let it be your wonderland." The guitar strummed louder. "I'm the Poetry Man...I make everything all right."

"Yeah, Sea World is expensive. I'd skip it," Sasha said.

"Where are you staying?" Russell asked.

"We were going to find someplace to tent camp on the beach, I guess," Holly said.

The group shook their heads.

"Oh, there's no sleeping on the beach here," Rachel said.

"If you don't have a lot of money, there's a hostel hotel ten minutes away. I think it's only five dollars a night."

I nodded. "We can afford that. So, what's the name?"

"It's Hi-Hostel—Point Loma."

"How long are you guys staying in San Diego?" Sasha asked, passing a joint to Christian.

Holly and I looked at each other. "I guess until we're ready to leave," Holly said.

Christian held the joint toward Holly. She turned to me, and I shook my head. I've smoked pot a couple of times in my life. But I've never enjoyed the feeling of not being in control. One night my sister's friends were over, they were smoking. I thought I'd be as cool as they were and took a few hits. Moments later, I couldn't even put my shoes on my feet. I held my foot up and then my shoe, but I couldn't figure out how to get my foot inside my shoe. I couldn't wait for the high to leave me. I never did get my shoes on, and I never smoked again. Although I pretended to inhale a few times after that when I was with friends. I don't do that anymore either.

"Ah, no thanks. Um, we had enough for the night."

Smoke floated out of Christian's nose and swirled out his mouth. "That's cool," he said. Russell slid the joint from between Christian's fingers.

"I'd love to stay here forever," I said.

"I read you loud and clear. That's why we're all still here."

The guitar strummed. "If you stay forever, you'll never find your way. So, you have to keep moving. There's no resting place along the road, so ride the wave that comes your way and live the free life every day. I'm the Poetry Man...I make everything all right."

The group continued smoking, and talking about their everyday lives. Holly and I watched and listened to what living in southern California was like. Around midnight, the beach patrol said it was time to go.

"Hey, Sandy and Holly, we'll be here tomorrow night, and every night if you care to join us," Russell yelled, dousing the flames of the fire with sand.

"Yeah, maybe we'll see you tomorrow," I said.

Moments later, we found the Hi-Hostel and checked in. Holly and I took the last two beds in a room with several beds. Some had wood headboards and some had velvet headboards. Holly and my beds had no headboard. They were just pushed against the wall. Curtains that were once white hung on rails, dividing each bed. At least the beds and bedding were clean. Holly and I closed our curtains on the sides but not the one between us. There were lockers to put our backpacks in and a table with towels, blankets, and extra pillows, and there was a balcony with an open window that let the cool night breeze in. It didn't take long for me to fall asleep, even with the snoring down the hall.

A complimentary breakfast of toast, bagels, and coffee was served in a large dining area in the morning. Holly and I toasted bagels, bought Cokes from the pop machine, and headed out for the day.

We were told that on a typical June summer morning in San Diego, the haze of the marine layer would blanket the sky until to sun rose and burned the layer away. It was cool in the morning as we strolled along the beach, stepping over the seaweed that washed up on the shore overnight. Holly and I dug up shells that were half-buried in the sand, and I kept a few of the white, unbroken clam shells as a souvenir.

We hung out at the beach that day. We swam and rode the waves to the shore and rolled around in the sand, the cool ocean waves washing over us—another perfect day. I fell in love with San Diego, the beach, the water, the food, and just hanging out, but I wished the water was warmer.

We heard other sunbathers talk about the seven La Jolla Caves twenty minutes north. It sounded interesting. There was only one cave accessible by land, and because of the changing tides, the other six caves could only be viewed by kayaking with a guide. We decided to save our money and skip the caves.

Later in the afternoon, a few feet away from us, a surfer ran out of the water carrying his surfboard. He dropped his board and started rubbing his lower leg. "I think I just got stung by a jellyfish," he yelled back to a few guys following him.

They dropped their boards and walked over to him. "Let's see, dude."

His lower leg was red and swollen. "Damn, this mother hurts."

"Yep. It looks like you got stung by a jelly," one of the guys said.

"Bro, you know what we gotta do, don't you?" Another one chuckled.

"No fucking way."

All the surfers laughed.

"Dude, relax. It's the only way to stop the pain." He pointed in the sand. "Grab that board and hold it up."

Two guys picked the surfboard up and held it waist high, which blocked our view. Something streamed down his leg. His friend stepped back and pulled his board shorts up.

"Oh my God, Holly, do you think he just peed on him?"

A couple of guys near us nodded their heads. "Yep, urine stops the pain."

"Eww. That's so gross." Holly grimaced.

"Ha, don't worry, Holly, if you get stung by a jellyfish, I'll gladly pee on you. I think."

We stayed out of the water the rest of the day.

After lunch, we walked further down the boardwalk and decided we needed to have a near-death experience by riding the wooden roller coaster built in 1925 because the tarantula and snake hadn't killed us. The ride was jerky, but the creaking of the old wood climbing slowly up the rails was the scary part. I closed my eyes as the roller coaster groaned, descending, and looping around the curves. I was afraid the roller coaster would break apart and send us flying into the ocean filled with jellyfish. "I think I need a drink after that ride," Holly said, wobbling out of the seat.

I held my hand over my stomach. "I'm with you. Let's go find a drink."

We walked by several restaurants along the strip with colorful umbrellas. "What do you think of this one?" Holly asked. We walked closer. All the Hi-top tables were filled with people and dogs—no empty chairs.

"I don't know. Let's try another one." We walked on. "You know they're going to know we're not old enough to drink."

"What will it hurt to try? If they say no, then we…."

"Get arrested.?" *Shit, Dan would kill me if I got arrested.*

"We can sit in the back where they won't see us."

At the next restaurant, the hostess greeted us. "How many in your party?"

"Just the two of us. Do you have anything in the back?" I asked.

She walked us to a small table next to the railing and handed us menus. "This is all we have open. Your waiter will be right with you."

Holly looked around, then back at the menu. "Want to split an order of nachos?" Holly asked.

"Okay." I leaned into Holly. "Ah, what drink are you going to get?"

"Hello, ladies, my name is Chad, and I'll be taking care of you today. What can I get you to drink?" He dropped a couple of cardboard coasters on the table.

Holly scanned the drink menu one more time. "I'll have a Strawberry Daiquiri," she said confidently.

"I'll have the same," I said, folding the menu. "And we'll have the chicken nachos too."

"Great. Two Strawberry Daiquiris. Can I see some ID?"

"Um…" I shrugged, and Holly looked down at the table.

"Okay, two Strawberry Daiquiri mocktails and one order of chicken nachos."

I handed my menu to Chad. "What's a mocktail?"

He smiled. "Mocktails are cocktails without the alcohol. I'm assuming neither of you is twenty-one."

We both shook our heads.

"So, you still want the Strawberry Daiquiri mocktails?"

"Yeah," Holly and I both said sadly.

Chad tucked the menus under his arm and walked away.

"This so-called mocktail better have an umbrella in it," I snapped. *Damn, we almost fooled him.*

We both giggled.

After dinner, Holly and I walked to the beach waiting for the sun to set. A guitar strummed; multiple notes hung in the air. We followed them. "Hey, guys," I said.

The guitar played. "Sandy and Holly are back. They know if they're hanging with us, they won't need any Prozac. I'm the Poetry Man…I make everything all right."

Russell waved us to sit. We sat close to the glowing embers of the flames crackling in the night air, casting shadows across everyone's faces. Everyone from last night was back, plus a new guy.

"This is Trevor," Russell said pointing to a dark-haired man wearing a white puka-shell necklace. "Trevor, my man, this is Sandy and Holly from Chicago and Breckenridge."

"How's it going," Trevor said with a head nod.

"Hey, Trevor," Holly and I said at the same time. It was hard to tell what kind of guy Trevor was. He seemed pretty mellow.

Russell settled in the sand. "So, where did you girls venture off to today?" Russell asked.

"We hung out at the beach...."

"Until some guy peed on his friend's leg."

"Oh, a jelly sting," Russell's voice sang out. "Those hurt like hell!"

"Yeah, if you see something white floating next to you, get away fast," Christian said.

"You girls care for a beer?" Russell asked, reaching into the cooler.

"Yeah, sure," I said. Holly nodded her head.

"Dude, grab me another," Trevor said, holding his empty bottle up.

Russell popped the caps off a couple of Coronas. "Here ya go."

Holly and I tipped our bottles. "Thanks."

"It's a perfect night tonight. No wind, no bugs, just peaceful zen," Rachel said. She leaned back, gazing up at the sky out over the ocean. "There's absolutely no clouds tonight. You can see every star."

Christian, still wearing his sunglasses, slid behind Sasha. He pulled her into him.

"Dudes and dudettes, does anyone know all the constellations?" Trevor asked.

Christian pointed. "Big Dipper right there."

"Little Dipper over here," Sasha pointed.

Those were the only ones I remembered. And the only ones I could see. Russell, Trevor, and Sasha rattled off a few more constellations, but I couldn't tell one group of stars from another. So, I nodded my head as they pointed them out.

Rachel tore open a plastic bag in front of her and pulled a package of marshmallows, a box of graham crackers, and chocolate bars out.

"Ah, dude, s'mores," Trevor said.

"I only have a couple of sticks, so we'll have to share," Rachel said.

"Okay, ladies first." Russell handed a stick to me, Holly, and Sasha.

"None for me," Sasha said. "I have my dessert right here." She rubbed Christian's leg next to her. Christian smiled and kissed the back of her head.

Oh my God, who would pass up s'mores? But I guess if I could snuggle with someone special in the moonlight, I'd pass on s'mores too...maybe.

Rachel slid a marshmallow on top of her stick and passed the marshmallows, graham crackers, and chocolate to Holly and me. We roasted the marshmallows over the fire. The flames flickered at the sugar coating of the marshmallows.

"Hey, Sandy, how did you like the Hi-Hostel last night?" Russell asked.

"Um, it was okay. We were in a room with, what, Holly, four other girls?"

"Yeah, there were about four others. We haven't really met them since we are in and out."

"Can't complain. We had a bed and shower for five dollars, and—"

Sasha nudged my arm. "Girl, your marshmallow is on fire," she shouted, laughing.

"Oh, crap." When I pulled my stick out of the fire and shook it, the flame grew around the marshmallow. I shook the stick harder one last time. The charred, flaming marshmallow broke loose from the stick and flew at Trevor's face. "Oh my God, Oh, my God." I jumped up and ran toward him, tripping over his legs. I fell on top of him, knocking us backward in the sand. I reached over to grab the marshmallow from Trevor's forehead, but Trevor had already pulled it off. I sat up. "Are you alright?"

"Trevor, man, you were on fire." Russell laughed.

Everyone laughed but Trevor and me. I climbed off him and noticed the melted marshmallow in the sand next to him. I could smell burned hair. Trevor's left eyebrow was half-gone, and he had a deep-red mark on his forehead.

"I'm so sorry...I...I...."

Christian tossed Trevor a cold beer. "He'll be okay. Right, Trevor?" Trevor held the beer bottle on his forehead and then twisted the cap off and guzzled it.

"Don't worry, Sandy, he probably won't even remember what happened tomorrow," Rachel said.

I sat down next to Holly. She smiled. "Nice one."

I clasped my hands around my knees and stared into the flickering flames. *I can't believe I just did that. I hope Trevor doesn't sue me because I don't have any money or anything. But, oh, God, please forgive me. I didn't mean to hurt Trevor.* "I'm so sorry, Trevor."

"Chill, girl, it was an accident," Russell said, rolling a joint on his leg. He licked the paper and twisted the ends.

"Yeah, a funny accident," Sasha said.

"Trevor, dude, you okay?" Russell asked.

"Yeah, man, pass me that joint, dude."

"Coming your way, man," Russell said.

The guitar strummed. "Catch on fire, and feel the burn. Ride the wave of life, washing you away, making you new again. I'm the Poetry Man...I make everything all right."

How does he do that?

Marijuana smoke hovered in the air, intermingling with the smoke from the fire.

The crackling of the fire was the only noise. Then, the crew took turns smoking the community joint, except for Holly and me.

"Hey, has anyone played never, have I ever?" Holly asked.

Rachel and Sasha giggled.

"What's that," Christian asked.

"Well, the first person makes a statement about something they have never done, like, "Never have I ever done this...." Then the players who have done what the person said will drink or take a shot of...whatever. If nobody has done what the person said, nobody takes a drink, and the person making the statement takes a drink. So, in the end, the person who drinks the least will be the winner."

"So, the person who drinks less is the winner? Why, because they never did anything?" Christian asked.

Russell laughed. "I'd call that person the loser. Because you gotta live a little."

Russell and Christian hi-fived each other.

"Okay, who's going first," Sasha asked.

"I'll go," Christian said. "Okay, never have I ever…seen a flaming marshmallow fly through the air on a hot summer night."

Laughter filled the windless night. Everyone took a drink of their beer.

"Very funny," I said.

Trevor cleared his throat. "Never ever have I been hit with a flaming marshmallow."

Nobody took a drink, except Trevor. I held my head in my hands. *Okay, I don't want to play this game anymore.*

The guitar strummed. "Start again tomorrow. Wake up with a purpose. A time when things go wrong, it's our light and not our darkness, so don't let fear become your master. You need to be strong. I'm the Poetry Man…I make everything all right."

"Sandy, never have you ever…?" Russell asked.

I thought for a few seconds that seemed like hours, staring at my feet. *I'm such an F-up. I'm glad my mother wasn't around to see what just happened. She probably would leave me again, except I didn't do anything wrong the first time—except being born.* I closed my eyes. I thought about my mother with a burning cigarette hanging from her lips, weighing marijuana on a scale that sat on our countertop every weekend. Then there were the large garbage bags filled with pot hidden in the back of her closet, kind of like my secret of who my mother was hidden inside of me. My gut tightened. Many nights when I was alone in the house, I was afraid someone would break in and steal her pot. Sometimes I wish they had. Then, her secret and my secret would be gone. I never told anyone what was going on at my house because I didn't want to be the person to send my mother to jail. I guess her words "children are to be seen and not heard" had paid off for her.

"Okay." I rubbed my hands on my legs. "Never have…I ever," my voice shook, "told anyone that my mother…is a drug dealer." There it was. I finally told my biggest secret on a sandy beach in California, sitting around a campfire with strangers in the moonlight. It was a secret no more. The hard surface surrounding me finally cracked, and I let out what was buried so deep inside. A heaviness left my body. *I'm not an F-up…she was.*

Their eyebrows lifted, there were long pauses. Nobody took a drink.

Holly touched my knee. "You okay, girl?"

I took in a long deep breath and nodded, then swallowed a sip of beer.

The guitar strummed.

Everyone turned to listen.

"Sorry, I got nothing."

"Wow," Rachel said.

"No judgment, people," Russell said.

"I'm sorry. I didn't mean it like that," Rachel said.

"It's okay. I'm okay." But I wasn't okay. Inside I was crying—poor little me. It was a sadness I'd carried around for many years. Most of my friends thought my mother was so cool because she partied and they could party with her and buy pot. I didn't think she was cool at all. And so many times, I wondered if my friends were just hanging around because of her. They were fakers. *I hate fakers.* I needed a mother, not a drug dealer.

Everyone took a drink of their beer, except me. My shoulders straightened; I sat a little taller.

The guitar strummed. "We live our lives then one day die. What's the reason? I'd like to know why. Do we come back as someone else and live in another soul? Or do we just go to a big black hole? Let's not worry. What will be will be. We should live our lives knowing, one day, our souls will be set free. Sandy, a phoenix rising from her mother's ashes, when she gets knocked down she gets right back up again." the Poetry Man shrugged his shoulders. "Sorry, nothing rhymes with ashes. I'm the Poetry Man…I make everything all right."

Holly and I left before everyone else. The strumming of The Poetry Man's guitar played 'Here Comes the Sun.' That's one constant thing. The sun was always there behind the dark clouds. You can't see it, but you know it's there. *Poetry Man, I will get back up again and again.*

ELEVEN

Sea Boy — Want Boy

The next day, we drove across the two-mile Coronado Bridge to Coronado Island. So many multi-colored towels, blankets, folding chairs, and umbrellas were propped in the sand along the sparkling white beach that you could see for miles.

Coolers divided the sun bather's territory while Coke bottles were nestled in the sand, straws bobbing up and down inside. Girls in bikinis and tanned, shirtless guys in board shorts that reached their knees were everywhere on the beach.

We spread our towels out on the beach. Young kids splashed in the water, and dolphins dove in and out of the water further out. Military planes flew overhead.

I turned facing Holly and pointed. "Check out those guys over there."

She sat up. "What guys...?" Her eyes widened. "Whoa. Nice."

"I know. What do you think they're doing?"

"Working out. Kind of?"

"Let's move closer."

We walked closer and unrolled our towels out a few feet away. Then, on our bellies, elbows in the sand, we rested our heads in our hands.

There were six of them: two black, one Hispanic, and three white. Two of the guys towered over the others, and they were all good-looking.

Their arm muscles bulged with every push-up they did. After finishing their push-ups, they ran short sprints—kicking sand as they slid into their turns. The two fastest had a runoff. The Hispanic guy yelled, "Three, two, one, go!"

Two of the guys took off sprinting back and forth. They were neck and neck. And then one pulled ahead of the other. Cheers erupted from the others. The guy from behind grabbed the leader's lower leg at the last turn, taking them both down.

They started to fall. Holly and I backed away on our knees but still got showered with sand.

One of the guys fell at my knees, face-up on my towel.

He smiled. "Sorry, Ma'am," the one standing said.

"I'm not sorry," the fallen one added. His crystal-blue eyes sparkled in the sunshine. "I couldn't have planned it any better."

I smiled. "I'd ask if you were okay, but it looks like you're more than okay. My name is Sandy." Holly nudged me. "Oh, ah, and this is Holly."

"Who are your friends?" Holly asked.

The fallen guy waved to the others. "I'm Lance Corporal Edwards."

Ah. Military. No wonder they all have extremely short haircuts.

I leaned into Holly and whispered. "They're Marines. Real Marines."

She smiled and nodded her head.

Lance Corporal Edwards rose to his knees. "This is Lance Corporal Thomas, Williams, Ross, Garcia, and Washington." "But you only need to remember my name." He smiled with satisfaction and winked.

"Ah, do we have to salute you?"

"No, Ma'am. You don't salute me. I work for a living." They laughed. "Only officers are saluted." Lance Corporal Edwards stood and brushed the sand from his board shorts. "Can we interest you ladies in a few beverages?"

"Yeah!" Holly said. She stood and grabbed her towel. "Let's go."

I grabbed my towel, and we followed them down the beach. Two Marines flanked Holly, and my crystal-blue-eyed Corporal Edwards escorted me. We stopped and joined a few people sitting around a keg of beer buried in the sand. Garbage bags of ice surrounded the keg. Most everyone looked a few years older than Holly and me. On the side, their name-engraved camouflaged duffel bags rested in the sand.

"New recruits, Edwards?," one of the bare-chested Marines asked.

"Nope. We just met them on the beach. But, oh, my God, when our eyes met, I was knocked off my feet." He rested his hand over his heart. "My heart went pitter-patter."

I turned to Holly and saw her rolling her eyes.

"The Marines could use a few fine women like you," another physically fit, bare-chested Marine said. He pointed over to a couple of girls. All the girls had their hair pulled back in tight buns. Whisps of hair fell, framing their tanned faces.

I sat next to the girls. "You guys are Marines too?" Holly joined me.

"We sure are," one said.

95

"How long have you been in? Ah, I mean a Marine?"

"First year for both of us," said the other one.

"Do you like it? Is it hard?"

"I won't lie. Boot camp was a bitch. But, I'm hoping all this hard work will make me a better person. I want to make something of my life."

"We're getting our orders soon," The other girl said.

"Where are you guys going to go?"

"We won't know until the day we ship out."

"How long will you be gone?" I asked.

"A couple of years." Two of the girls fist bumped.

"Wow." *I wonder what that would be like, to go away for two years.*

"Are you even a little afraid to go so far away…and fight?"

"The Marines train you for every possible situation. But unfortunately, most of us women won't see much combat."

"Which is BS because I want to kick ass and take names."

All the girls agreed. They were up for the task of kicking ass.

One of the girls stood and yelled. "Girls, the water is waiting." They got up and ran to the waves. They were so powerful and strong. *I bet they could kick some ass.* "Holly, they could be Cactus Girls." Holly nodded as we watched them attack the waves until they disappeared underwater. *I think I could be a kick-ass girl.*

Corporal Edwards slid next to me and handed me a beer.

"What are you doing tonight?"

"I'll be over here," Holly pointed where the other Marines were and walked away.

"Um, nothing much. Holly and I usually eat at the taco truck. *Because it's cheap and good.* And then we hang out on the beach. We met some guys and kinda hung out with them."

"Well, how about hanging out with me tonight? I'll take you to a nicer place—not a taco truck for dinner."

"Holly has to come. I won't leave her alone." *We leave together...We stay together...We come back together. NO, I'm not leaving you at the party by yourself! If you got to go to the bathroom or outside. We all are going to the bathroom or outside! Period!*

"Yeah, that's cool. It looks like Holly is making friends with Corporal Thomas. I'll ask them to join us." He waved them over. "How about dinner tonight? Us four?"

I stood up and walked over to Holly. We stepped away. "Are you okay with this?"

"Yeah, sure. It's just dinner, right?"

"Yeah. No taco truck tonight. What do you think about Corporal Thomas? I don't want to make you go if you don't want to."

"No, I'm fine going. He's kinda cute."

"Just cute? He's a rock."

"I know, right? Are you okay with Corporal Edwards?"

"Yes, most definitely." My heart was racing. *I think I just found my future husband. He can take me away. And I thought I was only looking for a geode. Maybe they're both rocks. But not like a geode. Or maybe they are geodes. The creepy gray guy said it's what's inside that is special.*

"So, girls, what's it going to be? Dinner or not?" Corporal Edwards shouted over to us.

We walked over to them. "Yeah, we're good."

"Great. Where can we pick you guys up at?"

"We're staying at the Hi-Hostel in town," Holly said.

"All right, we'll pick you guys up at six thirty."

Holly and I left around three o'clock to get ready for our date. When we got back to the Hi-Hostel, I dug through my backpack, pulling my clothes out. I held my tops up to my

97

nose and sniffed. *Eww,* I threw them on my bed. "Holly, I have no clean clothes to wear tonight." *Why didn't I wash these yesterday?*

Holly unzipped her backpack. "I've got a clean shirt you can wear." She pulled a shirt out of her pack and tossed it to me.

"Are you sure? What are you going to wear?"

She held up another tank top. "I have this one. Unless you want to switch with me?"

"This one will be fine. How come you have so many more clothes than me?"

Holly shrugged. "I don't know. I guess I overpacked."

I dug down further in my pack. *Ugh, I have no clean underwear too.* I plopped on the bed.

"What's wrong?"

"I don't have any clean underwear either."

Holly laughed. "Neither do I. We have plenty of time to wash them out in the sink and dry them outside before we have to go."

We washed our undies out in the bathroom sink and hung them outside on our balcony's ledge.

Holly pulled the blanket back on her bed. "I'm taking a nap. How about you?"

"I think I'll jump in the shower first before it gets busy."

There were a few shower gels that someone left in the shower. As the water cascaded down my body, I emptied one into my hand, and a hint of jasmine filled my nose. *I'm going on a date with a Marine. He seems like he likes me, but what if I like him too? He lives here, and I live in Colorado. How would that work? And after our date tonight, would I see him again?* I thrust my face into the steaming shower to calm my fluttering stomach. After showering, I towel dried my hair, wrapped my towel around me, and hurried back to our room. Holly was already asleep.

Yeah, maybe a nap will be good. Still wrapped in my towel, I climbed into my bed and closed my eyes. Curtains flapped in and out of the open balcony door. Outside, a dog barked, and loud Spanish music played. I held my pillow over my head. *This still isn't working. I can't sleep.* I got up and walked out to the balcony. Music was coming from apartments across the alley with fire escapes zigzagging up the sidewall. Through an open window, a young woman held a baby in her arms as it cried. *The baby probably couldn't sleep either.* I looked down. A woman stood holding a rope clothesline in her hand and a laundry basket at her feet, talking to someone who I couldn't see. I shuffled back to the bed. A blast of wind swept by. Then, out of the corner of my eye, something flew in the air and then fell. *What was that? What just fell?*

I ran to the balcony ledge and looked over. "Oh my God. Holly! Holly, wake up!"

"What? What is it?"

I ran my hand through my wet hair. "Oh my God, I can't believe this just happened."

Holly hustled out on the balcony. "What? What?"

We stared over the ledge. Our underwear was hanging in the tree branches below.

"Great. Now, what are we going to do?"

"Maybe we can ask the people below if they could help get them out of the tree," Holly said.

"I am not going to ask someone to get my underwear out of a tree. They're gone for good...I guess."

At six twenty-five, Holly and I were outside waiting for Corporal Edwards and Corporal Thomas. They pulled up right at six-thirty on the dot. Our Marines were dressed in casual khaki shorts and short-sleeve button-down shirts. Holly and I were in our best shorts and tank tops, minus underwear. "Sorry, we don't have anything fancier. We weren't planning on going out for dinner, ah, like this," I said, climbing into his Dodge Ram pickup truck. Holly and her Marine jumped in the back seat.

"Hey, no worries. You girls look great," my Marine said. We drove to the boardwalk, and they stopped at the Beach House Grill. Corporal Edwards held the door open for us. "After you, ladies," he said with a grin. After a short wait for our table, we were seated outside. Three-foot glass partitions separated the restaurant from the boardwalk and kept the sand from blowing in. Our two Marines held our chairs for us when we sat. I've never had a guy do this. I wonder if they learned this from the military or home. Either way, it was a nice touch. The sun was still out, and a cool breeze swept through, occasionally gently kissing our skin. The Marines ordered spicy wings and BBQ ribs. I debated ordering a salad because that's the ladylike thing to order and not get messy sauce all over your hands and face, so I ordered the pulled pork sandwich. Holly ordered the shrimp ceviche and a dinner salad. The guys ordered beers, and Holly and I ordered Cactus Cooler mocktails. After dinner, we wandered over to the Tiki Bar and sat on the couches near the fire pit. Corporal Edwards slid his arm around my shoulders. "Are you cold?"

Oh my God, he's making a move. "Ah, no, I'm fine. It's perfect out here." *This is a perfect night. Eat your heart out, JD. I don't need a cowboy anymore. I've got my Marine, and I'm in love. I think I can finally forget about JD now.*

At sunset, we strolled along the beach in the moonlight. I glanced back at Holly and Corporal Thomas who were walking a few steps behind us. We walked and talked for about an hour, and then Corporal Edwards's fingers brushed against my hand, and then our fingers curled around each other. A shiver ran through my body. *I think he likes me.* I turned slightly and saw Corporal Thomas reaching for Holly's hand, but she slipped it into her front pocket.

We kept walking. Neither Holly nor I said anything.

Corporal Edwards stopped and stepped closer to me, pulling me into him. He gazed into my eyes, and then his lips met mine. *Wow, this is so nice. A kiss on a beautiful summer night on a California beach with a good-looking Marine. I'm in heaven.* Our lips separated.

"You know it's our last night here. We're shipping off tomorrow morning. So, if you girls want, we could go somewhere a little more private. There's a hotel down the street." Corporal Edwards said.

Neither Holly nor I said anything. I closed my eyes. "*Wait…What?* My knees buckled. *Oh, my God, I can't believe he just asked us that.*

Corporal Thomas brushed Holly's hair from her shoulder. "How about it, Holly?"

My heart pounded as Corporal Edwards hands cupped my face, and he lowered his head toward my neck. "So…maybe we could…."

Holly stepped between us and snapped. "So, what? Maybe we could what?"

Behind us, Holly and I heard, "Corporal Edwards and Thomas, are you scamming these two girls?" Holly and I looked back at a couple of girls walking down the beach a few feet away. Both Marines' mouths fell open. *What is that all about?*

"Trying to get lucky again, boys?" One of the girls asked as they kept walking. My eyes widened.

"If they tell you that this is their last night here, run the other way. They're just looking to get laid," one of the girls shouted.

I stepped back. "Really? Is this a game you guys like to play?"

I pulled in a long unsteady breath and let it out. "I don't play games. Little boys play games."

Holly marched over to me, nodding her head.

The Corporals were silent. Corporal Thomas stepped behind Corporal Edwards.

"I can't believe you were going to do this to us. What did you really think was going to happen? Did you think we were going to fall for your sad story about shipping out, and how you're going to be sooo lonely?" I shouted at Corporal Edwards.

Holly pulled my arm. "Let's go, Sandy."

"Wait a minute, Holly." I walked over to them, swung my leg back, and kicked sand at them. "There! Take that, jerk."

I wanted to kill them, but I had given up killing.

Holly and I got back on the boardwalk and started walking back to our hostel. "What a bunch of jerks," Holly said.

"Did they really expect that we'd jump in bed with them just because they bought us dinner?"

"I'm surprised they bought us dinner first," Holly said as she laughed.

"What's so funny?"

"You sure showed them when you kicked sand at them."

I stretched my arms out and giggled. "Yep. Don't mess with me. I'm a Cactus Girl."

A half mile further down the beach, a guitar strummed. "Guess who?"

The flames from the fire lit up everyone's face as we approached. "I can't believe you kissed Corporal Edwards," Holly snickered.

"What? Who were you kissing, Sandy?" Russell asked, sitting cross-legged in the sand.

"Oh, nobody."

"Yes, she kissed Corporal Edwards," Holly said again.

"Ugh, shut up."

Rachel giggled. "A Corporal, huh?"

"You found yourself a few good men, did ya?" Sasha asked.

I plopped down in the sand. "I don't want to talk about it." Holly sat next to me.

Russell patted my knee. "All right, let's change the subject. We're glad you're back. After the last time, we were all together, I realized that we don't know each other very well. We like to learn about people we meet. So, I think we should share some stories." Russell looked around. "Um, Sasha, we'll start with you, if you don't mind."

Sasha sat up on her knees. "I'm an art student. I create art. Art opens your mind." She raised her hands, her fingers popped open. "And art brings out one's creativity. Art also tells a story and draws people into critical thinking," she finished with her hand resting on her chin.

"Whoa, that's pretty deep, Sasha," Trevor said.

"Your turn, Trevor," she said.

"Should I stand or stay seated?" Trevor asked.

Russell's eyes rolled. "Just say it Trev."

103

I couldn't help but stare at Trevor's half left eyebrow and red blister on his forehead.

"Okay. Well, dudes, I'm a sound mixer. I work at a recording studio. I mix instruments, sounds, and lyrics. I guess you could say I create art too. Musical art."

Russell pointed at Rachel.

"I do nothing. My parents are on my back to go to school or get a job, any kind of a job. But I don't want just any kind of job. I want one that I'll love doing. That's all."

"Hear that," Trevor said, clapping his hands.

Russell looked around the group. "Christian."

"Ah, Russell and I are trying to start up our own skateboard business. We're designing and building skateboards in my parent's garage."

"Pretty cool, dudes," Trevor said, nodding.

"Holly?" Russell asked.

I looked at Holly, she turned to face me.

"Um, I just graduated from high school and came here to explore with my bestie." She grabbed my arm. "But, I'm not sure what I want to do next, but part of me doesn't want to go back to Chicago."

I glared at Holly. *What's going on? This is the second time Holly said she doesn't want to go back home.*

"Your turn, Sandy," Russell said, pointing.

Everyone has such cool jobs, except me. I want a cool job. Maybe I should make something up that sounds cool. That will never work. Holly would call me out.

"Ah, um, I do nothing right now." *Do I really need to know now what I want to do with the rest of my life?* "Everyone else has cool jobs." *I got nothing.* "I'm kinda thinking about going to beauty school in September…maybe, but I'm not sure. I

104

mean, I like messing around with my hair and makeup, so maybe that's what I should do. Is that a cool enough job?"

"Yeah. That would be a cool job," Sasha jumped in. "You can work your own hours, do makeup and hair. I pay my girl who does my dreads a lot of money. You'll love it. You'll get to create art with hair."

The Poetry Man strummed his guitar for several seconds. "I'm the Poetry Man...I make everything all right."

I tuned out for a few minutes, still confused about what Holly said. *I wish I could read her mind.*

"Well, now that we all know each other a little more, we can take a little piece of everyone's story with us as we travel through life, where ever life takes us."

The guitar strummed. "You can't change the weather, nature, or your past, but how you perceive them and live with them will form your future fast. So, dream your thousand dreams with a brand-new heart, bury all the crap that happened in your past...be your sunshine...for tomorrow could be your last. I'm the Poetry Man...I make everything all right."

My head nodded. Holly tapped my knee with her hand. "Come on. We should start walking home before the hostel doors lock."

"You girls aren't walking back by yourselves, are you?" Christian asked.

I stood up. "We got a ride here from the Marines, and we left them, so, yes."

Trevor sat forward. "I can take you back."

"Are you sure?" Holly asked.

"Yeah, totally."

Trevor's car was an older blue Pontiac GTO that had seen better days. Under the streetlight, I could see that the paint was faded, and the door handle on the driver's side door was missing. I jumped in the back seat, where a dark blanket covered in dog hair was stretched over the torn seats, and Holly climbed in the front. Trevor cranked the ignition. It didn't start. "Damn, you're going to give me trouble tonight, huh?" He cranked it again. Trevor slid out of the car and opened the hood. "Holly, slide over in the driver's seat, and when I tell you to turn the ignition, press on the gas pedal and crank it."

Holly leaned her head out the window. "Where's the key?"

"There is no key. Just turn the ignition, he yelled from under the hood."

I leaned forward. *Oh great. Is this even Trevor's car? Dan would kill me if I got caught in a stolen car.*

"Go!" he yelled.

Holly pressed her foot on the gas pedal and turned the ignition. Click, click, click, then the engine roared.

"Got it! Woohoo." Trevor jumped back in the car. "Here we go."

I slid back and searched for the seat belt—There wasn't one. "Hey Trevor, how do you start a car without a key?"

"It's easy. You bypass the ignition."

"So, why don't you have the key?"

"I lost it years ago."

I'm sure this is his car. Who would steal this?

The following day, I found a phone and called Karen. The answering machine picked up again. "Hey, Karen, we made it to San Diego. It's sooooo nice out here. The weather is perfect. It's hot, but the ocean is kind of cold. Holly and I are staying in a hostel. There's, like, four other girls in the same room with us, but it's okay. We aren't around there much, and we're always at the beach. We eat cheap tacos from taco trucks, and we met some people on the beach. We hung out with them around a campfire for a couple of nights. One guy calls himself the Poetry Man. He plays the guitar and makes up poetry when he talks. It's weird, but some of his poems are kinda thought-provoking. They make you think about life.

"Then, we drove over to Coronado Island and met a couple of cute Marines. But that didn't work out so well. I think those were the guys you warned me to watch out for. They were jerks. But I met a couple of girl Marines. They looked pretty tough. Maybe I'll join the Marines. What do you think? Oh, I forgot to tell you I almost killed a guy with a flaming marshmallow. We were making s'mores, and my marshmallow caught on fire and then flew off the stick and landed on his forehead. He's okay, though. He's just missing half of his left eyebrow now. The worst thing about this trip is I haven't found any geodes. I doubt I'll find any in California. Maybe I'll find one in Yosemite or when I get back to Colorado. I'm going to look when I get home. There's probably a geode right in my backyard. It's crazy how every time I call you're not home. At least you know I'm alive and okay. I know you talked about me going to beauty school in September, and I'm seriously thinking about it, but I just don't know if it's right for me. All the people we meet have cool jobs. Is being a beautician a cool job? How do you know what the right thing to do is? I'm learning a lot from the people we're meeting. *Oh, my God, I feel like all I'm doing on this trip is searching for something, searching for geodes, and what I want to*

107

do with the rest of my life. I wish I had a phone number you could call me back on. I'll keep trying. We are off to LA and Hollywood next. Bye."

Why isn't Karen home when I call her? What's she been doing? Did she tell me they were going away and I forgot?

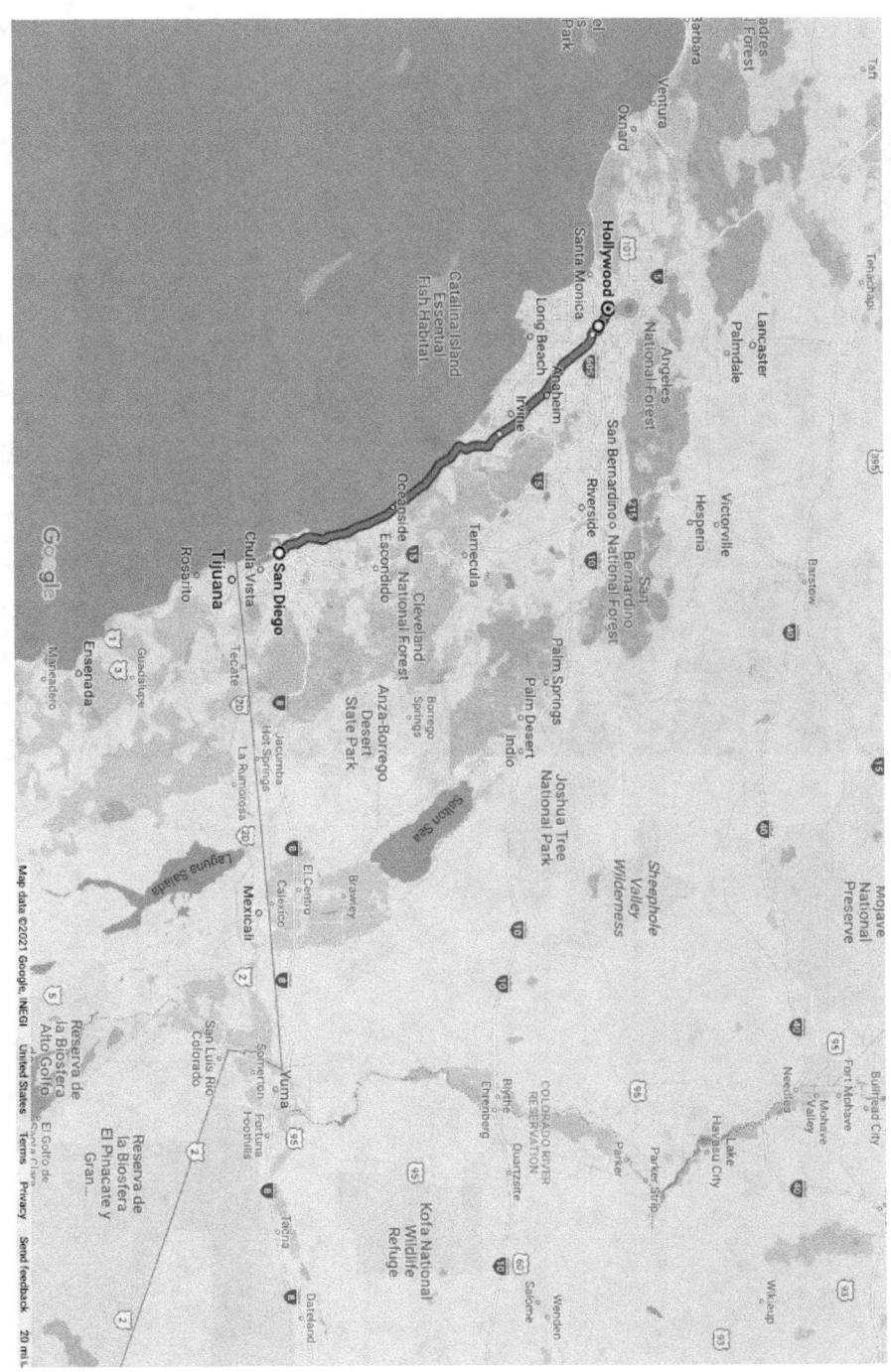

109

TWELVE

This Is LA

After four days beaching it in San Diego, we headed north to Los Angeles on the San Diego Freeway. Several times, cars were at a standstill. The traffic was horrible. We drove two hours and a hundred twenty miles along the ocean, passing signs for Huntington Beach, Catalina Island, and Long Beach. We took the ramp toward Santa Monica Boulevard, drove into Beverly Hills, and then turned down Rodeo Drive. On both sides of the streets, tall palm trees lined the road, along with white Mercedes, black BMWs, shiny silver Bentleys, bright red Porsches, and yellow Ferraris. At the stoplight, a woman dressed in a beige linen pantsuit and red spiked pump heels strolled in front of our car with a full-size brown poodle wearing a red beret. The sunlight sparkled on the woman's watch and necklace and the dog's diamond collar and harness.

"I don't think we belong here, Holly." *Or maybe they don't belong here?*

"No shit, and neither does that poor dog. Did you see how it was dressed? His clothes probably cost more than ours."

Down the street, a car pulled out. I pointed. "Oh, there's a parking spot, Holly."

Holly nudged in, parking between two sports cars. We got out and walked a few blocks.

We stopped in front of a clothing store. I had never heard of the brand, but it looked like a classy designer store. I walked to the door. "Let's go in here, Holly." Inside, two security guards the size of retired linebackers flanked the entrance. I smiled. They did not.

Everything in the store was locked behind a glass enclosure. I peered through the glass to read the price tag on a basic white camisole top. I half-whispered. "Holy shit, Holly, do you see the prices on these shirts? What are they made from, gold cotton?"

A saleswoman with pursed dark wine-colored lips projected her wish that we were not welcome. "Can I help you…?" she asked.

I waited for her to finish her sentence, but she didn't finish. "Ah, no, we're just looking," I said.

She walked away, pointing to the security guards.

I leaned into Holly. "Do you think they call them salespeople in a high-end store like this?"

"No. They call them bitches."

I looked down at my shorts and tank top that I bought at Target before our trip. "I don't think we're welcome here." *Or maybe she thinks we're going to steal something.* I slid my hand in my front pocket and held my lip gloss. *Maybe she knows that I stole a lip gloss from the store when I was eleven.* I felt so guilty after I stole it. I hardly used it. Days later I threw it away.

"Yeah, let's go." *I like my Target store way better.*

Three minutes later, we were on Santa Monica Boulevard. On every street corner, vendors waved arrow-shaped signs advertising maps and tours of homes of famous movie stars.

Holly pulled over. "How much for the tour?"

"Forty-five a person." The man wearing dark sunglasses continued waving his sign, "Yes…or no, yes or no?"

I shook my head. "How much for a map?"

"Five. Yes or no, yes, or no," he shouted.

I pulled a five-dollar bill out of my pocket. "Sold," I said, handing the guy a five-dollar bill.

A tour bus turned the corner. "Follow them, Holly."

Holly ran a red light so we wouldn't lose them. We followed behind the open-air bus, pretending we knew where we were going.

The tour bus slowed. "Look at the map and tell me where we're at."

I fanned the map open. "I think Julie Andrews' house?"

"From *The Sound of Music*?"

"Yep."

"Next."

We drove down a few more blocks. I pointed. "Okay, I think this is Carol Burnett's house."

Holly leaned over me, looking out my window. "You can't see anything behind the gates and bushes."

"Let's just drive on our own and look at all the houses and then move on."

"You mean mansions."

Next Stop, Hollywood. We strolled a few blocks along the Walk of Fame, where famous movie stars and anyone with anything to do with the movie and music business had their names engraved on bronze stars laid on the sidewalk. The Walk of Fame stretched for fifteen blocks.

Street performers dressed as Batman, the Joker, Catwoman, Spiderman, and Superman all wanted us to take pictures with them for a price. As soon as we said we had no money, they hurried on to the next tourists.

On Hollywood Boulevard, we looked up at the famous iconic Hollywood sign crisscrossing the sky in front of us.

"We need to hike there," Holly said, pointing.

When we got back to the car, we drove up the winding road, following the signs to Griffith Park. We parked and found the trail to the sign. The fresh pine scent of the longleaf pine needles from the evergreens covered the path, which reminded me of Breckenridge.

The closer we got to the sign, the harder it was to see. "Some people say the Hollywood sign is haunted," I said.

"Haunted by who?"

"In the book Dan gave me, it said in the 1930s, a struggling actress named Peg Entwistle climbed to the top of the letter H on the sign and jumped to her death. She was only twenty-four."

"Wow, that's crazy. I've never heard of her."

"Me neither."

"So, she didn't become famous for her acting, but she's now famous for how she died? That's so sad."

They say Peg Entwistle's spirit still roams the hills around the sign. She left a suicide note which read: "I am afraid. I am a coward. I am sorry for everything. If I had done this a long time ago, it would have saved a lot of pain." Peg Entwistle came to Hollywood looking to become a star, trying to make her dreams come true like so many others before her.

After our hike down from the Hollywood sign, we drove to Venice Beach. Along the boardwalk, chainsaw jugglers juggled, break-dancers spun and flipped, and guys and girls were selling kisses to the gathered crowd. A young rapper waved to Holly and me. Music was blaring out of a portable CD player on the ground.

"Hey, pretty ladies, how about buying a CD to support an up-and-coming artist."

"How much?" I asked.

"Ten dolla."

Holly shook her head. "No, we don't have ten dolla."

"Aww, come on. I'm going to be famous one day. You'll see."

I want to be famous someday.

"All right all right all right, then eight dolla."

We both shook our heads.

"Okay, just because you're both so pretty, I'll give you a special price of five dolla, five dolla. Come on. Someday my CD will be worth lots of money."

"I guess we could use some new music for the rest of the trip."

"All right, five dolla." I pulled five singles out of my pocket and slid the CD into my backpack.

"Thank you, thank you so much, pretty ladies. Come see me when I'm famous." He stepped away and yelled to people passing by. "Who wants to support an up-and-coming rapper?"

Further down the boardwalk was Muscle Beach, an outdoor gym, and not too far from that was a skate park for skateboarders. Kids of all ages and adults rode the curved walls and flipped over rails. We passed a tattoo shop and peeked in. A man standing in the door waved to us. "Come on in, girls. Come check out my artwork." Tattoos covered his whole body. It was hard to tell where one started and the other ended. "Are you girls looking for a tat?"

"Ah, no," I said.

"Maybe," Holly said.

"Really? You want a tattoo?"

Holly shrugged. "Why not?"

"What would you get?"

"I don't know. I'll know when I see it."

I looked over Holly's shoulder as she flipped through the sheets of artwork displaying colorful butterflies, angels, dragons and snakes, tigers, and even a tattoo that said "MOM." *No way would I ever get a tattoo with "MOM" on it. But maybe if I did get "MOM" tattooed on me, she would never leave me again.*

Holly stopped. "Oh, I like the tiger."

Of course, you do. "It's kinda big, though."

"I can make it smaller," the tattoo guy said.

I flipped through a few sheets. "How much for a small one?"

"For you, one fifty."

I took a deep breath.

Holly brushed by me. "See anything you like?"

"Um, not really." *If it's going to be on my body forever, I want something that has a meaning to it. Maybe something that will remind me of what's important in life. I wonder if they have a tattoo of a dreamer?* "Besides, we don't have enough money anyway. Right now, I'd rather spend my money on a cheap hotel and have a comfortable bed to sleep in tonight. How about you? See one you like?"

"Not really. I guess I'm not ready for a tattoo either." Holly handed the sheets to the tattoo guy. "All right, let's go find a cheap hotel."

On the pier walking back to the car, we found a fortune teller machine. The mannequin inside wore a red and gold scarf wrapped around its head. We stepped closer. Her gold hoop earrings started to swing. "For just one dollar, I will tell you your future, words of wisdom, or grant you a wish."

"Do you want to do it, Holly?"

"You go first," she said.

I pressed the red button. Nothing happened. "How does this work?"

"Feed the machine and then close your eyes. Concentrate on what you want, and then you'll be surprised."

"Oh shit. The machine just answered me. How did it do that?"

As I slipped a dollar bill in the slot, a hand reached out and grabbed it. Beams of light shot through her eyes. Music started to play, and then a ticket emerged from the machine. I pulled it out.

"What does it say?" Holly peered over my shoulder.

"It says, 'Break free from the people who hold you back.'"

Holly snatched the ticket from my hand. "What do you think that means?"

"I don't know." I pulled the ticket back and shoved it into my back pocket. "Your turn."

Holly pulled a dollar bill from her pocket and fed it into the machine. The music played, and flashes of light beamed from her eyes again. A ticket spit out. Holly grabbed it.

"Are you kidding me?"

"What, What?"

"It says, 'A move away will bring big changes your way.'"

I yanked her ticket out of her hand. "What does that mean? A move away?"

Holly plucked it out of my hand. "I don't know. But I'll let you know if I decide to move."

That was freaky. This has to be made-up stuff. How could a machine like that tell your fortune or future? I wonder if any of this stuff could come true.

On the way to the car, I kept thinking about my fortune. "Break free from the people who hold you back." *What's that supposed to mean? What people? How do I break free?*

After we got to the car, we headed toward California Highway 1 to look for a cheap hotel. I pulled our new CD out of the case and slid it into the player. "Let's see if this rapper is any good." A screeching noise filled the car. "Holly, I think your CD player is broke."

"It better not be. She pulled to CD out, blew on it, and put it back in. It wailed again. "Oh my God, what is that noise? Is that a baby screaming?" Holly asked.

"It's that CD we bought from that up-and-coming rapper."

The screaming continued. "It's either a baby or a cat," Holly yelled over the noise.

I advanced the CD. More screams and crying. It continued to the end. "This is unreal. It's nothing but a crying baby. What the hell, he ripped us off."

Holly laughed. "You mean he ripped you off."

"Ugh! If he thinks this is art, he will never be a famous rapper. He's a scammer, not a rapper." I ejected the CD and threw it out the window. *Scammed again. What a waste of money.*

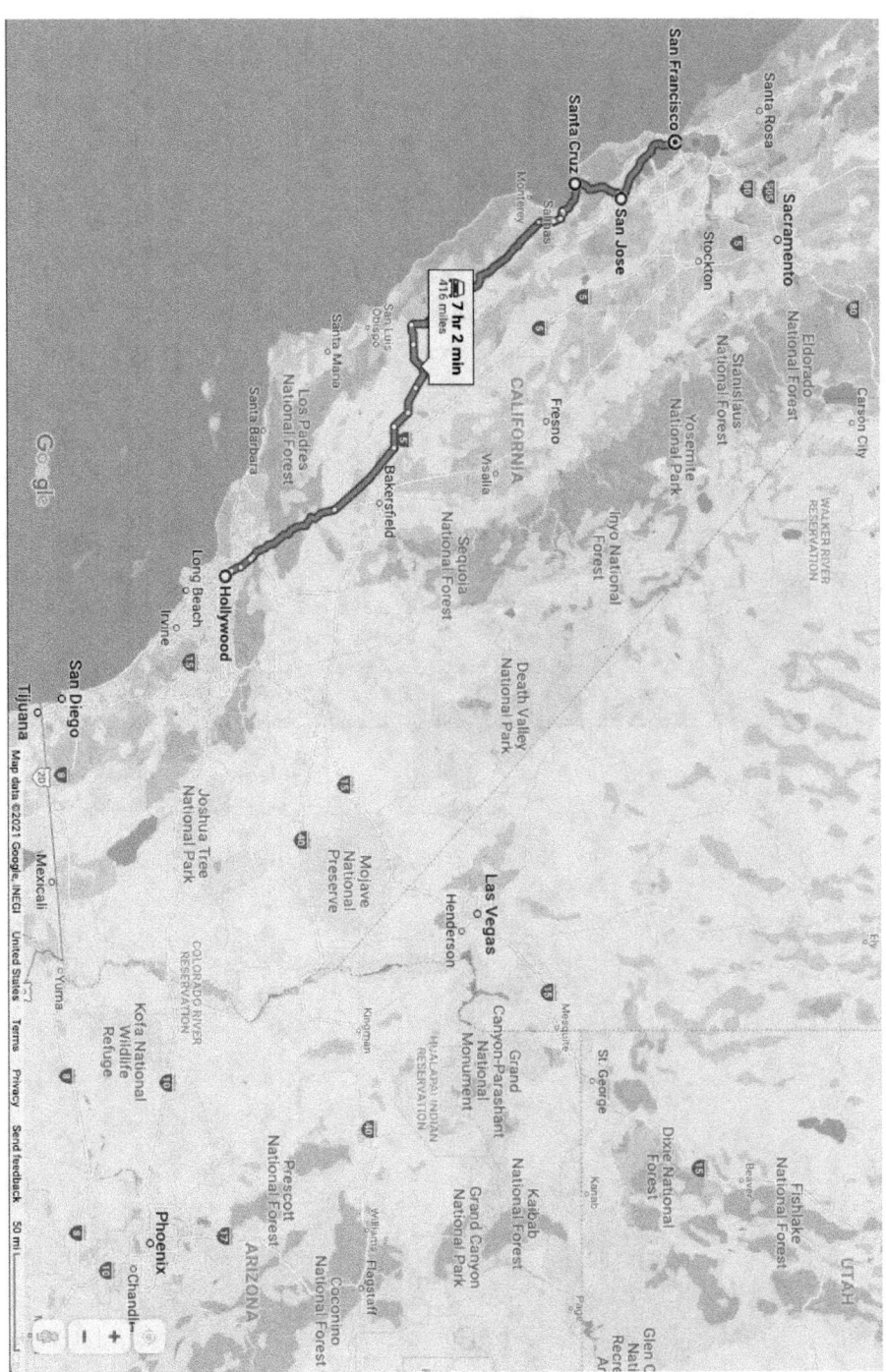

THIRTEEN

Never Pick Up a Hitchhiker

Later that night we found a cheap motel for forty dollars a night with air-conditioning, a TV, and a hot shower a few miles down the highway. The next morning the hotel served a complimentary continental breakfast. After we ate, we stuffed a few apples, oranges, and wrapped day-old bagels in our backpacks for later.

We left Venice Beach and drove to the 1 North. At the street corner a few feet from the onramp, we waited for the light to change. Across the street, a guy who didn't look much older than us was sitting on the curb, a backpack slung over his shoulder. A white surfboard rested on the concrete wall behind him. His golden-blond shoulder-length hair sparkled in the early morning sun. He held a handwritten sign above his head. "NEED A RIDE TO SANTA CRUZ."

I looked over at Holly, who was watching him too.

"What do you think?" Holly asked.

"Really? Pick him up?"

"How dangerous could he be?"

"I don't know."

We both kept staring at him.

"We've got plenty of room," Holly said.

"Yeah."

"And maybe he'll pay for gas," Holly added.

"Could work. But…."

"But nothing. There's two of us and one of him."

"And he has a surfboard."

Holly laughed. "I don't think a surfboard could be used as a weapon. And if we make it there alive, we'll ask him to teach us how to surf."

"I kinda like how you think. I guess he's not much bigger than us. I think we could take him down if we had to. We're the Cactus Girls. We can take down a surfer."

"Agree?" Holly asked.

"Yeah. Agree."

When the light turned green, Holly drove across the street and rode up to the curb. He held his sign up in our direction and nodded.

We both nodded back.

He opened the back door. "You headed to Santa Cruz?"

"Yep. Hop in."

He tossed his sign on the side of the road. Then slid his backpack inside next to the cooler and bungee-corded his board to the roof of the car. "I'm so amped you dudettes scooped me."

I looked over at Holly, and we both laughed. He sounded just like Trevor. *Trevor must be a surfer too.* I turned toward the back seat. "Hey, no problem. My name is Sandy, and our driver for the day is Holly."

"Ah…My name is Kai."

Holly pulled back into the lane and headed onto the Highway 1 ramp. "What kind of name is Kai?" she asked, looking into the rearview mirror.

"Ah... It's a cool surfer name that I call myself. Maybe one day, I'll be a famous surfer, and I'll brand myself."

I turned toward the backseat. "What's in Santa Cruz?"

"Ah, dude, it's only the best bitchin place to surf the bomb waves."

"Aren't there places to surf here?" Holly asked.

My eyes scanned him from head to toe. "Yeah, we saw a ton of surfers here."

Kai slid up to the front seat. "Dudes, Santa Cruz has the history. It's the original "Surf City." At one time, Huntington Beach was named "Surf City USA." But Huntington has too many junkyard dogs. Santa Cruz, it's the bomb, and don't let anyone tell you differently, dudettes." He fell back.

Holly and I giggled. "What's a junkyard dog?" Holly asked.

"Aww, dude, a junkyard dog is an amateur! They're kooks."

I laughed back again. "English, please."

"Ah...a junkyard means they got no style. Kooks means they're rookies." He leaned over the front seat, glancing back and forth between Holly and me. "You dudettes surf?"

Holly looked over her shoulder. "No. We tried in San Diego, but...."

"No wave action," I said, winking over at Holly.

"Yeah, I hear ya. Santa Cruz has the big guns. That's where they host the Mavericks in the winter."

"What's the Mavericks?" I asked.

Kai rested his elbow on the back of the front seat. "Ah... it's the biggest surf competition in the US, man. Bros come from all over the world to surf the big guns. So, what's your story, dudettes?"

"We're on a month-long vacation out West. We're going to Santa Cruz too and then see what's in San Jose and then to San Francisco and then over to Yosemite."

"Aww, dudes, I've been there a few times. Yosemite has big gun rocks, man. It's bitchin."

He sank back into the back seat. I turned and leaned over the front seat. "Do you hitchhike a lot?"

"Ah, only when I need to get around."

"Aren't you afraid to hitchhike?" Holly asked looking in the rearview mirror.

"Ah...not really. Maybe. Sometimes. I call it getting scooped. I was so stoked when you dudettes rolled up. Do you dudes scoop hitchers often?"

"Ah, no. This is the first time," I said.

Kai tapped his fingers on the cooler lid. "So, aren't you dudettes afraid that I might be a psycho killer or something?"

I glanced over at Holly and smiled. "Well, what are the chances that there would be three psycho killers in the car at the same time?"

We all laughed.

Kai's eyes held a puzzled look. "Wait. What? Three?"

Holly looked in the rearview mirror again. "I've got my eye on you, Kai."

"You're fine," I said. "So, where are you from, Kai?"

"From around. You know, here, there, nowhere in particular."

Once we were out of the city, we rolled the windows down. The fresh, salty ocean air rushed in, blowing our hair. Loose papers we had thrown in the back fluttered around in the car. Rocky cliffs on our left led down to where white-capped ocean waves crashed along the shore as Holly navigated the sweeping curves, my stomach jumping with every turn. "Hey, Holly, pull over at the next overlook. I need a break." She found a lookout spot, and we got out and walked over to the cliffside. Below the ragged points, paragliders hung in the air, free-flying, and circling in the sky.

"Far out, man. Gliders."

I turned to Kai. "Have you ever done this?"

"No way, dude. See how they are getting the juice from the air?"

"So, the air makes them go higher up?" Holly asked.

"Affirmative. The more juice, the higher they fly."

The gliders floated like colorful birds, like free birds. My stomach settled from the motion of the curves, but then adrenaline swept throughout my veins. *You can't cage a bird that needs to fly.* I closed my eyes and pictured them sailing away, far away to somewhere new. *Maybe life is more about the journey than the destination.*

We continued north along Highway 1. The view of the vast ocean never left our side. In Pismo Beach, we stopped for gas.

The back door opened, and Kai stepped out. "I got this." He filled the tank and paid.

"Thanks, Kai," Holly said.

I don't think a psycho killer would pay for gas before killing us.

We drove through the small town of San Simeon, where the Hearst Castle is, and then through Monterey Bay. An hour later, there was an exit sign for Santa Cruz. I looked back. Kai's head was resting on the cooler, Eyes closed.

Psycho killers wouldn't fall asleep either. I don't think.

We drove into the coastal town of Santa Cruz and dropped Kai off at the Santa Cruz pier entrance. "Hey, dudettes, thanks for scooping me."

"No problem," Holly said.

Kai grabbed his backpack and unsnapped his board from the roof of the car. "Be safe, dudettes."

"You too, dude," I said. *Thanks for not killing us.*

"Oh, and thanks for the gas," Holly shouted.

Kai waved his hand without turning around. He walked off toward the water with his board tucked under his arm.

Holly found a free parking spot on the street a block away, and we walked back to the pier jetting out over the ocean. The ocean rose and fell as surfers in black wet suits bobbed up and down on their boards. I thought I saw Kai paddling out where the other surfers were.

At the end of the pier, dozens of sea lions barked as they shaded themselves on the wood rafters below. A few feet away, Sea otters floated on their backs, some with baby otters nestled in their arms. Periodically they dove in the water and then popped up, spitting in the air through their long whiskers.

Along the row of souvenir shops on the pier, neon green, orange, and pink tee shirts, and sweatshirts with 'Santa Cruz' on them decorated the windows. Racks of brand name flip-flops that I couldn't afford covered the back walls, and stuffed sea animals overflowed in a basket near the cash register. I knelt to dig through the basket and pulled a stuffed black baby sea otter out. *Kelsey would love this. But I had no extra money to spend on souvenirs for myself, let alone Kelsey. When I get a good job, I'll be able to buy everything I want. And if I can't find a geode, I'll buy my own someday.* I've only been gone a couple of weeks, and I'm missing Kelsey already, my little buddy who looked up to me and asked a million questions. I liked being part of her family that I wasn't born into but found along the way. I reached in the basket and found a bigger sea otter. It must be the mother. I nestled the baby next to her in the basket. I don't know if it was the mother sea otter, but at least the baby wouldn't be alone. I hope whoever buys one of them will see them together and buy them both. The baby still needs its mother.

Holly and I found a carryout window at a restaurant and shared an order of freshly caught fish-n-chips and Coke. After eating, we walked through a parking lot where vendors sold wind chimes with tiny rust-colored bells and feathered dream catchers made from driftwood that had once been tangled in brown seagrass and had washed up onto the shore. I whispered to Holly, "I can make something like this from branches in my backyard."

She nodded and laughed.

There must have been hundreds of boats docked out on the piers. Some boats had sails, others were yachts that were as big as a small house, and some were bigger than big houses. We walked out on the piers where private fishing boats sold their leftover daily catch of fresh seafood. Some buyers came prepared and filled their coolers with fish, packing them with ice. Others carried off whole live crabs that tried to scale the clear, slippery walls of their plastic-bag prisons half-filled with seawater. Overhead, screeching seagulls swooped in, thrusting their wings as they fought to snag the floating remnants the fisherman threw back after they cleaned their catch.

The Santa Cruz Beach Boardwalk stretched quite a distance along the waterfront, and it had a retro amusement park with games and rides for all ages. We didn't want to waste our money on rides, but we found a candy shop and bought some homemade fudge. Holly bought peanut butter fudge, and I bought chocolate. We shared the fudge while we people-watched along the boardwalk. "Hey, Holly, I think we should go find the campground and settle in before it gets too crowded."

Holly took the last bite of her fudge. "Yeah, I think you're right. Let's go."

When we got back to the car, I leaned over the front seat and grabbed the handle to the cooler. "Hey, Holly, you want a Hawaiian Punch?"

"Yeah, sure. I'll take one."

I pulled the cooler across the seat. Lying on the other side was a brown leather wallet. I reached around the cooler and picked it up. "Holly, I think Kai left his wallet."

She turned around. "What?"

I held it up. "Damn it. How are we going to find him?"

Holly reached back. "Give it to me."

I handed it to her, and she opened it. "Are you kidding me?"

I leaned across the front seat. "What, What?"

"His name isn't Kai," Holly said.

"What do you mean?"

"His name is Benjamin Birk."

"Benjamin?"

"Damn, girl, look at the picture. It's him. He's a fraud!"

I slid over the front seat. Holly handed me his driver's license. "It is him. He lives in Bel Air. We were just there."

"He's a fraud! He lied about his name and where he lives."

I handed his driver's license back to Holly. *Benjamin Birk.* "But why would he lie about his name?"

"Because maybe he stole someone's wallet."

I ran my fingers through my hair. "Or what if he killed someone and then took their wallet?"

Holly shook her head. "So, he's not a fraud, but a killer."

He still lied about his name. I hate liars…and killers.

Holly opened the wallet. "Sandy, there's, like, four hundred dollars in here."

"What? Holly, we have to go find him and give his wallet and his money back." *I would die if I lost that much money.*

"We're never going to find him. Besides, he lied to us and pretended to be someone else. So, we should keep it."

I looked out the back window. "Yeah, you're right. We'll probably never find him now. We should teach him a lesson about lying to people. We're the Cactus Girls, and nobody lies to us."

Holly started the car and drove toward the California Highway 1 North entrance to find the KOA Campground. Neither of us spoke for a few minutes.

"I guess we could mail his wallet back to the address that's on his ID," I said, breaking the silence.

"No. We're not doing that." She continued to drive.

Many moments passed.

"Holly…"

"I know." She turned off on the next exit and pulled back onto the highway going south. "But we don't have much time. We have to get to the campground before all the spots are gone."

FOURTEEN

Is He a Killer or Not?

We drove down the road where we dropped Kai off earlier and parked in front of a surf shop when someone pulled out of a spot. Holly turned the car off and turned to me. "Let's go find him. And if we find him, we find him. But, if we don't, we keep the money. Deal?"

"Deal."

It was late in the day, and surfers were emerging from the water. Holly held her hands around her mouth like a megaphone and yelled. "Kai. Kai."

I walked up to a surfer who was peeling his wet suit off. "Do you know someone named Kai? Um, he has blond hair, and he's a surfer." *Or maybe he's not a surfer, and he lies about that too.*

He laughed, shaking his leg loose from the wet suit. "All surfers call themselves Kai."

I showed him the photo on the driver's license.

"Nope, don't know him."

"Thanks anyway." I walked over to Holly, who was still calling his name. "Well?"

"Nothing."

"Lets' try calling his real name." We got closer to the ocean and both yelled, "Benjamin. Or Kai, whatever your name is." Still nothing.

"We can't stand here all day. He's probably gone," Holly said.

"Did he say where he was staying?"

"No. I don't think he mentioned it."

"Let's go then. We can take care of this when we get home."

We walked back to the car and got in. The door to the surf shop in front of us opened abruptly. "Come back when you have money, dude," The man said, pushing a guy out of the shop.

"Man, I have money. I just don't know where my wallet is."

"Holly, it's Kai. I mean Benjamin."

She jumped out of the car. "Kai?"

He looked up. "Whoa, dudettes!"

"Kai, you left your wallet in our car," I said.

Holly handed Kai his wallet.

"Whoa, man. Thanks. I was wondering what I did with it. Thanks, dudettes."

"Yeah, no problem," I said. "But you lied to us, Kai, about your name."

Kai hung his head. "Ah, yeah. I didn't mean to. Kai is kinda a nickname surfers use."

I stepped in front of Kai. "You know, we weren't sure we should have picked you up. We thought you were a nice guy." *That you wouldn't kill us.* I folded my arms across my chest. "And then you lied to us."

"Aww, man. I'm truly sorry. I didn't mean to lie to you. I really am a good guy."

I looked at Holly out of the corner of my eye.

Holly sighed. "What are you going to do now, Benjamin? Can we give you a ride somewhere? Maybe Bel Air?"

"Yeah, I lied about where I lived too. And after all this, you're still willing to give me a ride? I don't want to keep you from anything."

"No. You're not keeping us from anything."

"But we probably lost our camping spot for the night," Holly said.

"Aww, man, I'm sorry bout that too. Ah, you can crash at my place."

"You gotta place…here?" I asked.

"Well, yeah, it's my parents' house. And nobody's there, so you guys can crash there for the night, or as long as you want."

I looked at Holly. "Well?"

She pulled me aside. "What do you think?"

"I guess it would be okay." I looked over at Kai. "He may have lied about his name, but we've established that he's not a psycho killer so far."

"All right. We'll see what his house looks like first and then decide, if the place is a dump, we're leaving. And we're not sleeping in the same room with him."

"Eww. No, we are not going to sleep in the same room."

Six blocks away, we pulled into a long driveway. A golden house with purple trim rose high above all the other places on the block. A three-foot gold wrought iron fence enclosed the front yard. Holly stopped the car. "This is your house?" Holly asked.

"Yeah. It's Mom and Dad's house."

"I thought your driver's license had a Bel Air address?"

"My parents have two houses." Kai opened the car door. "Come on, let's go inside."

We grabbed our backpacks.

Walking up the wide concrete stairs that led to double full-glass front doors, I looked up and pointed. "What do they call the round things with a steeple on it at the top of the house?" I asked.

"They're called turrets," Kai said.

"How many turrets does this house have?" Holly asked.

"There's four turrets."

A purple plaque with gold lettering on the front of the house read

"1891 Golden Gate Villa. Queen Anne Victorian Built. Historical Landmark."

Wood wainscot walls and a mahogany staircase greeted us as we walked in. "I'll take you guys upstairs and find a room for you." At the second landing, a stained-glass window of a woman in a garden of exotic flowers stretched across the wall. *This is like the windows in a church I used to go to every Sunday with my grandmother when I was young.* A few more stairs and we had reached the second floor. Down a deep red-carpeted hallway, we passed several closed ten-foot-high mahogany doors. "How many bedrooms do you have?" I asked.

"We have ten bedrooms and twelve bathrooms." Kai stopped and opened one door. "Here's one room, and there's another across the hall." He opened the door across the hall. "Who wants which room?"

Holly and I peeked into both rooms. "What do you think, Holly? Should we stay in the same room or have our own?"

"I don't know. It would be nice to have a room to ourselves, but…."

"I know what you mean." I pulled Holly toward me. "But, should we stay together? What if he comes in and tries to kill us later tonight? If we're together, we can at least have a chance to fight him."

"Well, he hasn't tried to kill us yet."

I looked over at Kai. "I think he heard us."

"All the doors have locks on them if you're worried, Sandy," Kai said.

Unless you have a key, Surfboard Killer.

"And you'll each have your own bathroom."

"Okay." We both said at the same time.

Kai opened a closet door in the hallway and handed us soft, comfortable oversized white robes. Inside my room, I took off my clothes and draped myself in a total luxurious robe. When we were changed, Kai walked us down to the massive laundry room next to the servant's quarters. We threw our clothes in the washer and then shuffled along barefoot in our robes as Kai took us on a tour of the rest of his mansion. On the third floor, a penthouse overlooked the coastline and out across the city lights of downtown Santa Cruz.

"Is this your room?" Holly asked.

Kai laughed. "No. This is my parent's space. I live in the carriage house in the back." Kai winked at me.

A carriage house? That's probably where he kills everyone and hides the bodies.

Kai took us across the backyard to his carriage house. His place was cozy. A large-screen TV, a sectional couch, king-size bed, and a full kitchen and bathroom. "Are you guys hungry? I'm starved. How about pizza? I'm buying."

"Yum," Holly said.

I stretched out on the couch, pulling my robe across my legs. "Pizza sounds good to me too."

"What do you want on it?"

"Anything except anchovies," I said. Holly agreed.

Kai ordered one large sausage and one pepperoni pizza.

Holly sat next to me. "Kai, I mean Benjamin." Kai hid his face in his hands. "So, tell us the *real* reason you call yourself Kai?"

He glanced at Holly and then me. "Ah, man, I guess I call myself Kai to escape who I really am."

I swallowed hard. *Oh, my God, he's a killer.* I pulled my robe tighter around me and slid to the end of the couch.

"What do you mean by that?" Holly asked. "Who are you?"

"All right, I guess I owe you guys an explanation. Um...well, as you can see, my parents are wealthy. And I...I got tired of living in their shadow all the time."

I shook my head. "Most kids of wealthy parents would love living like this. You'd have money to do whatever you wanted. If I want anything, I have to earn my own money. Even when I was young, I had a paper route."

Kai jumped up and paced the floor. "It's not about having money and buying anything you want. My parents are used to having perfect people around them, and they expect me to be perfect too. Everyone in LA is an actor. Nobody is real. It's all pretend." Kai's voice quivered. He pointed to himself. "But I was real, and when I fucked up, it was real, and they don't want anything to do with me."

My mother was disappointed in me when I talked.

Kai sat down and rubbed his hands on his legs. "So, I became Kai, the surfer. And...."

And you're a killer?

"What did you do to fuck up?" Holly asked.

Kai hesitated. "Ah, I kinda…robbed a bank."

A smile spread across Holly's face. "Cool."

Great, a bank robbing surfboard killer. "Ah, how do you kinda…rob a bank?"

"It's a long story."

"We've got all night," Holly said.

Until he kills us. "Did you kill anyone?" I asked.

Holly shook her head slowly at me. I shrugged my shoulders. The doorbell rang. "Pizza's here," Kai yelled.

Kai walked back into the room and laid the pizza boxes on a table in front of us and poured us each a glass of root beer.

I took a bite of a pepperoni pizza slice. "Okay, get back to your bank robbery story."

Kai took two bites of his sausage slice. "A couple of years ago, my parents wanted me to work and earn my own money. So, after school and on weekends, I worked as a porter at a car dealership in LA."

Holly and I both grabbed another slice of pizza and leaned in.

"A service advisor who didn't like me, I guess I was a smart-ass punk, handed me a bank bag and told me to go to the bank and get some money for the cashier. So, I did, but what I didn't know was he put a note in the bag that said, "Give me all your money. I have a gun." I never opened the bag. And, I had no idea what the note inside said. I thought it was telling the teller how much money they needed for the cashier."

I watched his eyes as he told his story.

"Then what?" Holly asked.

"I walked out of the bank. But before I left, I stopped and bought a couple gumballs from the gumball machine by the front door and then drove back to work."

He ate a slice of pizza.

"Did you get caught?" I asked.

"Yes. The teller knew who I was cause I go there almost every day. The cops rushed into the dealership and into the service department where I was working. They threw me up against the wall and handcuffed me. They were shouting, "Where's the money?" I told them I gave the bag to Fred, the service advisor, and then they went to his office and cuffed him." Kai laughed. "I bet Fred shit his pants when he opened the bag and saw all the money in the bag." He ate another slice.

"Why would Fred shit his pants when he's the one who put the note inside the bag?" Holly asked.

"Ah, because he thought I'd look in the bag and read the note before I went in the bank. He tried to prank me. He should have gotten fired, but he didn't."

"Wow. Did you go to jail?" I asked.

"Yes, and no. First, the coppers took us down to the station and interviewed both of us separately, and then they locked us both up in a cell until they got the bank video. Fred kept saying, "It was a joke. It was a joke.""

"Some joke. You could have been killed," I said.

"And they just let you go?" Holly asked.

"Yep. The bank got their money back, and they couldn't prove that I knew I was robbing the bank. I guess buying gumballs saved my ass."

"Unbelievable," I said, shaking my head.

"And this is where I fucked up with my parents. The bank robbery was all over the front page of the newspaper the next morning. "BANK ROBBERY JUST A HOAX." Man, my parents were so pissed, not that I could have been killed, but because my name was in the paper for robbing a bank."

My eyes softened. *Maybe Kai's not a killer after all, especially when he could have been killed himself.* "But that wasn't your fault."

"I know, but I embarrassed my parents by robbing a bank and being on the front page of the newspaper. My parents are pretty important and well-known in LA."

Holly picked a piece of pepperoni off her slice and dropped it in her mouth. "Maybe someone will make a movie about it. It is LA, after all." Kai and I both chuckled.

After finishing the pizza, Kai scanned the TV channels and found the movie *Pretty Woman*. "I think you'll enjoy watching this," Kai said, and we settled in to watch the movie. After the movie, Holly and I went back to our rooms in the big house. Kai stayed in his carriage house.

Before bed, I filled a gold clawfoot tub in my private bathroom with warm water and bubble bath. I slowly slid into the hot water, covered myself with foamed bubbles, leaned back into the soft bathtub pillow, and closed my eyes. *This feels so nice. I would love to live here and have my own bedroom and a bathroom all to myself. I would take a bubble bath every night...yep, every night. I would be able to buy whatever I wanted, and I'm positive there would never be any moldy food in the fridge either. This would be great.* The warmth of the water softened my body and mind. *But, if I did live here, who would my parents be?* My eyes shot open. *Would they be like Kai's or like my mom and dad?* I closed my eyes again. A smile came to my lips. *Could you imagine if you could choose your mom and dad?* My heart jumped. *But then I guess moms and dad would also be able to pick the kids that they wanted. Ugh...This would not work out very well for me.* My mom wanted a boy, but she got me. I sunk lower in the tub. Bubbles and water covered my head.

In the morning, the rays of sun peeked through the trees, forming spots of sunlight on the emerald green carpet in my room. A knock at the door. "Rise and shine, girls. Breakfast is ready." I dressed quickly and opened my door. Holly was opening her door too. "Kai made us breakfast?" *Maybe he feeds people before he kills them.*

Kai had egg McMuffins, hash browns, and orange juice sitting on the table in the kitchen.

"Good morning, girls," Kai said.

"Good morning," Holly and I said in unison.

Kai sat down at the table. "So, are you surprised you're both still alive?"

Holly laughed.

"Very funny, Kai, or should I call you Benjamin?" I snickered.

"All right, no more thinking I'm a killer…."

"You, a Killer? Why would I think that?"

"And no more pretending you're someone you're not," Holly added, taking the last bite of her hash browns. "And by the way, you're both crazy."

"So, where are you girls going now?"

"We are heading to San Jose. Do you know the way to San Jose?" Holly giggled.

Kai rolled his eyes.

After breakfast, Holly and I packed our backpacks. "Thanks for letting us stay with you, Kai," Holly said.

"And thank you for the ride and bringing back my wallet." Kai picked up our packs. "I'll walk you out."

"Kai, can I use your phone? I need to call someone."

"Yeah, sure. You can use the one in the kitchen or the study."

I lifted the receiver on the phone in the kitchen. "This one is fine."

I dialed Karen's number. It rang five times, her answering machine picked up. "Hey, Karen, it's me. I'm checking in. Holly and I are leaving Santa Cruz. I think the last time I called you was when we were leaving San Diego. LA was so crazy busy. There are so many cars on the highway. We drove around to see some movie stars' houses, but we couldn't see anything. The stone fences and giant trees hid all the houses from the road. We went to Rodeo Drive, but everyone was so snooty, and we couldn't afford to buy anything anyway. Can you believe a plain old tee shirt was like one hundred twenty dollars? And then in Hollywood, we saw a lot of stuff you can't make your eyes unsee, like dogs wearing clothes and people dressed up as Batman. We hiked up to the Hollywood sign where Peg Entwistle climbed to the top of the letter 'H' on the sign and jumped to her death because she couldn't make it in Hollywood. That was so sad.

We heard about underground caves in La Jolla, which sounded cool, but we didn't want to pay to go on a tour. And then, well, don't get mad, but we picked up a hitchhiker on our way to Santa Cruz. He turned out to be pretty cool. He wasn't the psycho killer we thought he'd be. But anyway, he let us stay at his house last night. His house was enormous. It has a thousand bedrooms. Kai is his name, well, not really his

141

name is Benjamin, but anyway he bought us McDonald's for breakfast. Well, I gotta go. We're off the San Jose, and Holly is waiting for me in the car. Talk to you later, maybe if you ever answer."

FIFTEEN

We Don't Need to be Pretty Women

Holly and Kai were waiting for me outside. I slid into the front seat. "Thanks for letting me use your phone."

Kai leaned in through my window. "No problem." He pulled out his wallet and handed me four hundred dollars.

"What's this for?" I asked.

"Take it."

I pushed his hand away. He moved his hand back inside. "No, please take it. You came back to find me and return my wallet and money. Most people wouldn't have done that. You saved me the headache of having to replace my driver's license and credit cards. So, please take it."

Holly leaned over. "You don't need to give us all this money, Kai."

He tossed the money inside. The money scattered across our laps. "If you don't want it, then use it to save someone's life." He turned to leave. "Oh, and one other thing." He pulled a pocket knife out of his front pocket and handed it to me. "Someday, you might need this too, for protection." Before I could say anything, he was gone.

We drove east on California 1, music blasting, windows down, hair blowing. Twenty minutes later, we were in San Jose.

"Holly, what did you think about the movie last night?"

"*Pretty Woman*? It was good. Why?"

"Do you really think some guy is going to come along and take you away to a better place so you won't have to be a hooker anymore?"

Holly laughed. "Or a hairstylist? I don't think that would happen. But you never know."

"*Pretty Woman* was like a modern-day Cinderella story."

"Yeah, it was."

"And those saleswomen in LA kinda treated us like they did Julia Roberts," I said.

"But we're not hookers."

"But they still judged us." We sat in silence for a minute. "I think fairytales are bullshit." I glanced over at Holly. "Do you think people ever get to live happily ever after?"

Holly shook her head. "No, I don't. But I think we need to stop worrying about happily ever after and live happy each day."

I giggled. "Wow, pretty deep, Holly."

"Well, *we* don't need to be rescued. Cactus Girls don't need rescuing."

Sometimes I do.

"And if you just said to yourself that you need rescuing, you need to rescue yourself."

How did she know I said that?

SIXTEEN

Deadly Consequences

A billboard showing a black, red, and white multi-peaked house hung over the roadside. The black, hollowed eye sockets of a skull resting inside the outline of the black house pulled me in. "Hey, Holly, do you know what The Winchester Mystery House is?"

"No, what is it?"

"Um, if I knew, I wouldn't have asked you."

"Ha-ha. So, what is it?"

"It looks a little mysterious. And there's a skull on the house." *I think it's daring me to go.* "And it says guided tours daily. Do you want to go?"

"Is it a haunted house? Because I'm up for anything spooky."

I hate haunted houses and scary people. I don't like my heart racing, not knowing what's behind a door or around a corner waiting to jump out at me. I can't be afraid of a house. I mean, I'm a Cactus Girl. I killed a tarantula and scared a giant snake away. I can handle a house, even though there's a skull on it, which usually means death. But maybe death doesn't mean the death of a person, but the end of something that haunts you.

"I don't think it'll be gory like a normal haunted house. But, it does look interesting."

Holly followed the road to Winchester Boulevard and pulled into the driveway. The Queen Anne Victorian mansion stood seven stories high in front of us. I thought Kai's Queen Anne house was big, but this was enormous. We parked and walked to the front entrance. Inside the gift shop, a picture of the Winchester House hung on the wall. An aerial photo showed the multi-peaked red-roofed house, with many additions spread over an entire city block.

In 1884, Sarah Winchester, the sole heir of Winchester Rifles and Guns, was haunted by those killed by a Winchester. Sarah sought out a medium, who told her to build rooms to ward off spirits of the dead.

"Whoa, this is kinda cool," Holly said.

"Yeah, but it's thirty-nine dollars to get in."

"The 1 o'clock tour is about to start. Please have your tickets ready," a man wearing a red velvet cap bellowed from behind a red velvet rope stand.

Holly pushed me forward. "Let's get in line. We'll pretend we're with the others."

An older man next to me was holding tickets in his hand, and an older woman, a few steps behind him, was talking with a woman next to her. I glanced at him. "Hi. Do you come here often?"

His eyes widened. His sunken cheeks blushed.

"Ah, I mean, is this your first time here?"

He nodded.

"Ours too," I said, taking Holly's arm in mine.

The red-hatted man unhooked the rope and stepped aside. After a few people walked in and Holly and I followed, the man held his hand out for our tickets. Holly and I nodded toward the man I was talking to earlier and his wife, and we slipped in behind the couple in front of us. *This is so wrong.* I looked back at him, but he kept taking tickets from other visitors. The tour started in the foyer, which led to one of the forty-seven staircases. The tour guide recited the same history as the picture hanging in the lobby. "One of the mysteries of the Winchester House is that it has over ten thousand windows, some of which open to brick walls and open staircases. It also has two thousand doors that lead to nowhere." The tour guide took us from one crazy room to other haphazardly built rooms and up and down several staircases that led to brick walls.

I leaned into Holly. "Do you think this house is really haunted? This is kinda creepy. I can't believe she thought if she built all these rooms, it would ward off the haunted spirits. It wasn't her fault. She didn't kill anyone." *Are we all supposed to be responsible for what family members do? Could I be responsible if my mother sold pot to someone who got sick and died? I don't want to be like Sarah, and I don't want to be like my mother either. But then I just snuck into a house that is haunted by wrongdoing.*

The tour ended in the gift shop. There were racks and shelves of Christmas ornaments, books, and refrigerator magnets. "Holly, I think I need to buy something." I stopped at the circular rack. "Ah, like a postcard." I pulled one out that matched the billboard I saw on the way here.

"Are you feeling guilty that we snuck in, and now you have to make it right by buying something?"

"Yeah, maybe." *Oh, my God, I am feeling guilty. I'm haunted.*

Just like Sarah, she built rooms to right the wrong, and I felt like I had to buy something to right my wrongdoing.

We left San Jose and arrived thirty minutes later in San Francisco. The city of San Francisco was the home of many infamous earthquakes.

We pulled into a gas station, and while Holly was gassing up, I went inside and bought a couple of Diet Cokes and a bag of Fritos. I looked to see if there was a creepy gray man working behind the counter. Maybe he could tell us where all the geodes were. And why was it so hard to find them? There was no gray-haired man here, though. A younger man with glasses took my money and paid me no attention. On my way out, I saw a rack of brochures. I grabbed a few that showed things to do in San Francisco. I jumped in the car. Holly was waiting for me.

"Whatcha got there?" Holly asked as I jumped in the car.

I waved the brochures toward her. "Stuff to do in San Fran. Let's go see the Golden Gate Bridge first, then ride a street—"

A car horn blew long and loud. Holly looked in the rearview mirror, and I turned around to see who was honking.

"Get moving," a man shouted from his window.

"I think we should get going," I said.

"Some people are so impatient," Holly said, pulling out into the street. "Okay, which way are we going?"

"Um, I don't know. What street are we on?"

"How the hell do I know."

I grabbed the dashboard. "Whoa shit, that bus just pulled out in front of us. That bus driver didn't even look. He almost hit us. We could have been killed."

Holly laughed. "He wasn't that close, but he is much bigger than us, so he gets the right-of-way, I guess."

"Let's get to the bridge before we die. Take this exit toward the water. The bridge has to be there." I looked to my right. "Oh, there's a sign for the Golden Gate Bridge."

Holly weaved in and out of traffic. Buses and railed streetcars continued to cut us off, as well as people running across the street not worried about cars coming at them. Homeless people walked the streets, talking and singing to themselves. They were having quite the arguments with God and about God, and we should all repent. I rolled up the car window when we stopped at the light and turned away from them. Right before the light changed, Holly yelled and waved her hands. "No!, No. I don't need the window washed." Water sprayed from a bottle and a dirty rag swiped across the windshield. Holly honked the horn. "Move out of the way," she yelled out the partially open window.

After the window was completely smeared, the guy hurried to the driver's side of the car. He held his hand out. "Pay."

"Pay what?" Holly asked.

"Oh, my God, he wants us to pay him?"

Holly shook her head. "No!"

"What do we do?" I asked.

"I'm not giving him a dime."

The light turned green, and horns honked behind us.

He banged on the hood of the car.

I handed Holly the bag of Fritos. "Here, give him these."

Horns honked again and again.

Holly rolled the window down just enough to pass the bag out the window.

"Go, go," I shouted.

He grabbed the bag of Fritos, and Holly sped away. I turned around, and watched him throw the bag of Fritos at the car.

"That was crazy," Holly said. She turned the windshield wipers on and cleaned the smears away.

We crossed the famous Golden Gate Bridge, parked at the visitor's center, and walked to the lookout. A red steel bridge supported with cables spanned the San Francisco Bay. There were several lookout telescopes along the sidewalk. I slid a quarter into one and scanned the bridge. "Hey, Holly, I think there are nets below the bridge."

"What kind of nets and what are they for?"

I pulled away from the scope. Holly peered into the telescope while I opened the brochure and skimmed through it. "The brochure says they're suicide nets. They're there to deter people from jumping off the bridge and dying."

"Really? I can't imagine jumping off a bridge to end your life."

I looked out at the length of the bridge and how far down the churning ocean water was below. You didn't need a telescope to see that.

I'd never known anyone who committed suicide. A couple of my friends had been killed on motorcycles, and it was scary to think how one day they were here, and the next day they were gone. I never saw them again. I wondered if they'd known the day they got on the motorcycle was going to be their last? I had joked with one of them who was my best friend, that we'd grow old together, and when we were ninety years old, we'd sit in rocking chairs on a wraparound front porch. I thought we'd be friends forever. Looking at the bright red bridge was sad. I wondered if people who jumped got up in the morning planning for it to be their last day. I guess part of living was dying. And if you could choose to live the way you want, shouldn't you be able to die the way you wanted? Was it better to choose when you die, like jumping off a bridge, or wait until fate takes you?

I folded the brochure and slid it into my back pocket. "Hey, Holly, promise me something."

Holly stepped away from the telescope. "What?"

"That you'll never jump off a bridge or...."

"Oh my God! I would never do that."

"But you'd tell me if you thought about it, right?"

"I guess. Would you try and stop me?"

"Damn straight, I would. You're my backbone. I mean, you keep me strong." We both looked into each other's eyes. Her eyes filled with tears, same as mine.

"And I would keep you stronger. You'd tell me if you'd do the same, right?"

"I don't know. I mean, I've never thought about doing anything like that, but sometimes, I think one day I'll lose you." *And then I'd lose myself.* I swiped a tear from my cheek. "That you'll go away, and I'll never see you again."

"I'm not going anywhere, so, don't worry. But no matter what happens, we need to be here for each other."

"We will. I mean, I will because we're the Cactus Girls."

"Yep."

We quickly hugged.

Holly popped another quarter into the telescope. "What's on that island over there?" Holly asked.

"Which one?"

"The one with the buildings and a tower, and is that barbed wire?"

I pulled the brochure out of my pocket. "Ah, I think that's Alcatraz Prison?"

An older man standing near us wearing a black knit hat and dark sunglasses said, "yes, that's Alcatraz, also known as The Rock. Have you heard of Al Capone, George 'Machine-Gun' Kelly?"

"Ah, Al Capone," I said. Al Capone had a secret hideaway in a town near Chicago along the Fox River. It's now a restaurant. Bullet holes are still in the dark wood walls and low ceilings.

The man continued. "How about Alvin Karpis 'Public Enemy number 1' and Arthur 'Doc' Barker?"

Holly and I shook our heads.

"Well, they were the most famous prisoners at Alcatraz. You want to hear something else?"

We nodded.

"Okay, in the entire history of Alcatraz, thirty or so prisoners tried to escape. The ones who tried were either captured, shot, or drowned in the sea. However, in 1962, three prisoners did escape. They were John Anglin, and brothers, Clarence Morris, and Frank Morris." He held up three fingers. They were thick and rugged, and two were partially missing.

Our eyes widened. "Really? How did they escape and not get caught?"

He slid his hands into his front pockets. "The investigators believe they made a raft out of raincoats and made it to shore. No bodies were ever found, and nobody heard anything about them. It's still a mystery to this day if they made it to shore alive or not."

Why is everything such a mystery? "So, they could still be…?"

"Alive?" The man laughed. "If they made it to shore, yes, they might still be alive and walking amongst us right now.

But that was a long time ago." He slid his hat lower and nodded. "You ladies, have a nice rest of your day."

"Thank you, you too." When he was out of earshot I grabbed Holly's arm. "Oh my god. Holly, did you see his fingers? What if he's one of the prisoners that escaped? I bet his fingers were bitten off by a shark when he was in the water."

Holly laughed. "If he was, why would he tell us about it?"

"I don't know. Because he's creepy?" *I think I just met an escaped prisoner—with two fingers missing.* I turned to see where he went. He was gone. *He escaped again.*

Holly peered into the scope again. "So, what else is there to see?"

"All right, let me get my book." I pulled the book from my backpack and scanned through the pages. "Um, Lombard Street."

"What's that?"

"It's a zigzag street that's on a steep hill that you can drive down. It looks pretty cool with nice landscaped flowers and trees, or we could ride on a trolley car through the streets of San Francisco."

Holly walked over and peeked over my shoulder at the brochure. "A trolley car."

"Okay. Let's go find the trolley cars."

We crossed the bridge and drove back toward the wharf and parked. Before we hopped on a trolley, we stopped in Ghirardelli Square and bought some famous Ghirardelli chocolate. The old trolley car stopped at the corner. The bell clanged, and Holly and I jumped on. We sat on a wooden seat next to an open-air window. The trolley took us up and down and around the steep streets of San Francisco. It stopped at the top of Lombard Street so we could see the steep, zig zaggy one-block road. Every time the trolley stopped and started, the bell clanged. Next, we drove past the house where the movie *Mrs. Doubtfire* was filmed. It still looked the same as it did in the movie. Then to the famous Golden Gate Park.

Further on, we arrived at the famous Haight-Ashbury neighborhood. Hipster heaven—the birthplace of the hippie movement from the 1960s. Peace and love signs were everywhere. Long-haired barefooted guitar players leaned in doorways, singing, and strumming their instruments. Guitar cases sat open before them so people could drop money in as payment for their performances. Later in the evening, we found a hostel in the Castroville neighborhood in the heart of the Art District. Many homeless loitered on the sidewalks in makeshift houses made from cardboard boxes with plastic tarps sheltering them.

"I don't feel very safe here," Holly said. "We need to find a hostel or a hotel somewhere else, and I don't care how much it costs."

"I'm with ya. Tomorrow morning, when we get up, let's head to Yosemite. *I doubt I'll find any geodes in San Francisco. But I'm sure Yosemite will have geodes there.*"

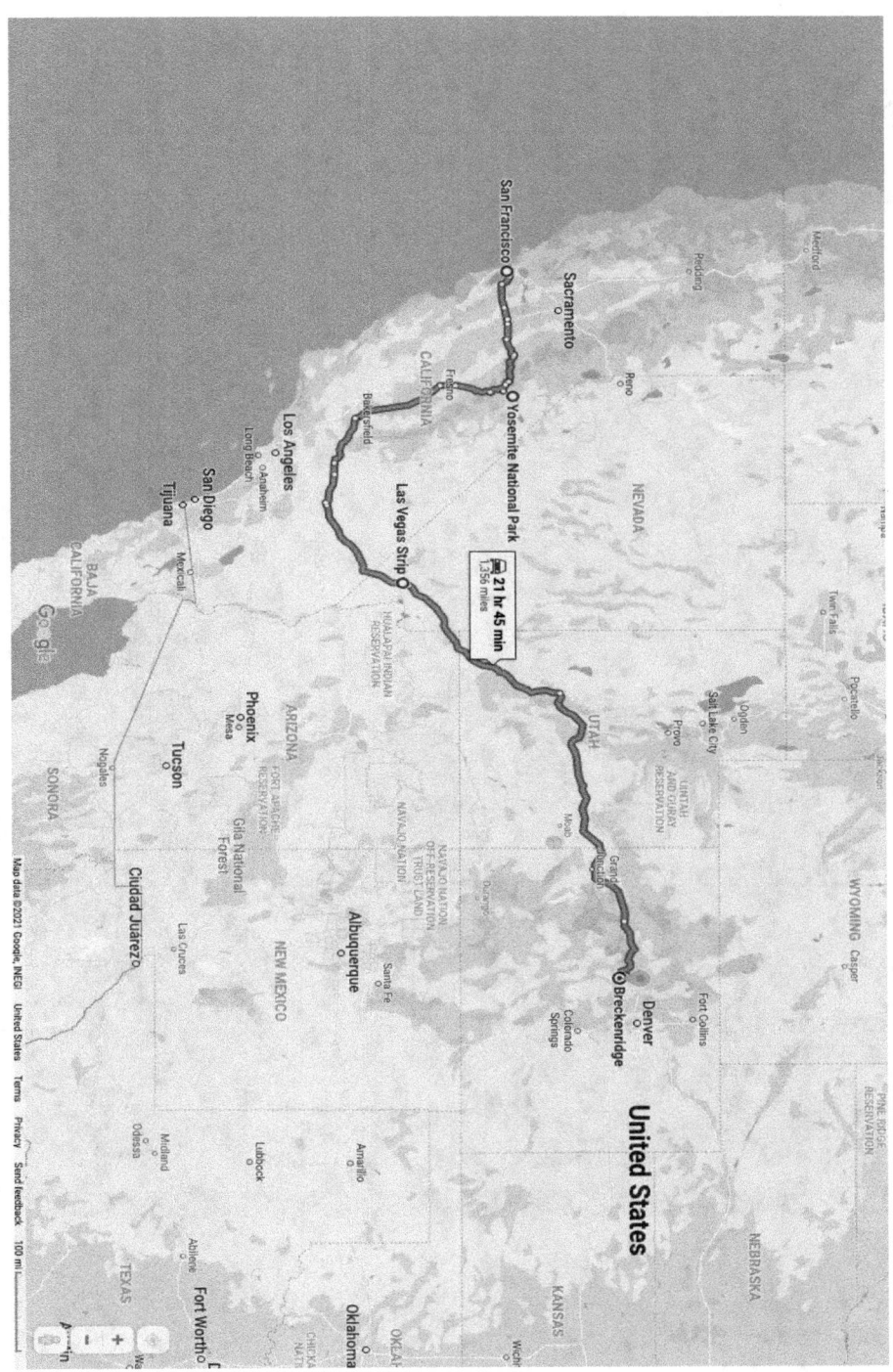

155

SEVENTEEN

Sometimes All You Need to Do Is Stand Up,
Clear Away the Dead and Renew

After Holly and I woke up, we mapped out our trip to Yosemite. *The land of the powerful granite.*

Yosemite was three and a half hours away, and as we drove east of the big city, the signs along the road were smaller and the traffic was lighter. The four-lane highway narrowed to two lanes, and then further away, it became one. We passed through almond orchards and small farming towns. Steep inclines along the road wound around the mountain, making my stomach rise and fall with every turn. Several times, I stuck my nose out the car window and breathed in the fresh pine air.

Cars drove by with families packed inside, luggage strapped to the roof. My eyes followed this one car, with a young boy's face plastered to the backseat car window. When he made fish lip against the glass, his breath fogged the window. "Holly, do you ever think about getting married and having kids?"

"Nope."

"Why not?" I asked.

"I'm too young. There are too many things that I want to do and places I want to go right now. What about you?"

"I guess I think about it sometimes." When I was younger, I pretended I had four kids. Two of them were twins. I took care of them and loved them every day. And then, other times, I thought about being married and not having any kids. Just my husband, just the two of us, and…. Nobody else. Silent moments passed. "How do you know you'll be a good mother, Holly? Do you ever think about that?"

"I don't think about it because I'm not ready to be a mother."

Why am I so fixated on being a mother? And worrying if I'd be a good mother?

Several more silent moments passed.

"Hey, you need to stop worrying about the motherhood stuff. My mom did a good job raising me. I'm not so sure about my sisters, but I'm good."

"Yeah, but I think my mother could have done a better job. I mean, what mother ties her daughter to the bedposts so she doesn't have to get up early in the morning and take care of her, and then leaves when she doesn't want to be a mother anymore?" *I don't want to be a mother. I'm afraid I'll do the same thing. Mothers are not supposed to leave.*

"Do you need a pair of scissors?" Holly asked.

"What? A pair of scissors?" *What is she talking about?*

"Yeah. A pair of scissors. You need to cut yourself some slack." Holly laughed. "You are going to be a great mom because you'll want your kids to have a better life than you had. And I doubt you'll do what your mother did to you when you have kids."

Yes! You're so right. My kids will love me because I will always be there to love them.

158

At the park entrance, giant redwood trees flanked the small brown wooden greeting station. "Oh, look, Sandy, they have a senior rate. Should I tell them we're seniors?"

"Ha-ha, very funny."

Holly giggled.

I handed my National Park pass to Holly, and she gave it to the park ranger dressed in a dark-green ranger uniform and a brown wide-brimmed hat. He handed Holly back the pass, a permit to keep in the car, and a map of the park. We entered a massive rock world blanketed by a forest of towering trees. Along the redwood tree-lined road, Holly and I had to tip our heads out the window to see the tops of the giant trees. A mile down the road past a wildflower meadow, a monster rock formation with a sheared-off side stood high, dominating the valley. I unfolded the map. "I think that's Half Dome," I said, pointing to the granite dome on the right. Three sides were smooth, and the other side was sheared off, making it look like the giant rock formation was cut in half. I pointed to the towering granite rock formation on the left. "And that's El Capitan. It says in the map that people scale El Capitan and climb all the way to the top, and they even sleep in hammocks hanging off the rock. And on Half Dome there are cables hikers can climb up to get to the top."

"Cool, do you want to climb up there while we're here?" Holly asked.

"Ah, no! I like to keep my feet firmly on the ground."

"There might be geodes up there." Holly snickered.

Oh great. They probably are all up there. "Well, I guess they're going to have to stay there then."

"Where's your sense of adventure?"

"I don't think I have to climb a mountain to find adventure, Holly."

We found Upper Pines Campground a few minutes later and set up our tent in the fourth campsite. Nearby, the Merced River tumbled over rocks that had broken away from the mountains hundreds or thousands of years ago.

After setting up our tent, we set out to hike the famous falls in the park, the Lower Yosemite Falls. Along the busy trail, we stepped over and around trees that had fallen and were left where they fell. Giant pinecones as big as our heads were scattered on the path, and we could hear the thunder of the falls a mile away. When we got to the lower falls, we stood on the wet wooden bridge watching the water from the upper falls crash onto the boulders of the lower falls. Sprays of water sent a fine mist glistening in the sunlight as it blew in the air. The falls forced the water to tumble over the rocks below, where the water continued under the bridge, cascading into white-capped rapids down into the valley.

A pool of water surrounded by boulders created a unique swimming hole. Holly and I climbed over the rocks and boulders to get close to the falls and joined the other tourists splashing in the pool of water. I wiggled my toes in the cold running water. Then waded in up to my calves and sat on a rock, where the water came up to my waist. At the edge of the falls, I scanned the rocks surrounding me. I jumped up. "Holly, I think I see a geode."

"Where?"

I pointed. "In that pile of rocks where those boys are playing."

"How do you know it's a geode from over here?"

"I don't know. I'm just guessing. But how do you know it's not?" I stepped up on a boulder, then hopped over to the next boulder that was half-submerged in the water, passing behind the boys. When I got closer to the edge of the boulder, I reached over to grab a rock the size of a football.

"Hey, be careful over there, Cactus Girl," Holly shouted.

"I will, but this damned rock won't budge." I pushed away several rocks of various shapes and sizes around it. "I think I got it." I grabbed the rock and pulled back. When the rock broke free, I stumbled backwards, bumping into one of the boys playing on the rocks behind me. The boy fell, hitting the boulder, and slipped into the water. "Help," he shouted.

Oh no. "Are…are you okay?" I yelled to him.

"My foot is caught. I can't get it out."

"All right. I got you." I placed my rock down on the boulder and waded in the water. When I got to the boy, I pulled on his leg, but it wouldn't move. A wave of water from the waterfall shot over both of us. The boy's head went under. *Oh my God.*

"Oh shit," Holly yelled and ran across the boulders to where we were.

Holly reached for him and lifted his head out of the water. I dove underwater and tugged on his lower leg. His legs suddenly kicked free, and he climbed out of the water.

"Check your foot and see if it's okay," I yelled to him.

He ran his hand along his foot. "It feels fine," he said.

I pulled myself out of the water. I was dripping wet. "Are you sure?"

He laughed. "I was just joking with you. My foot wasn't stuck. I just wanted to see if you girls would save me."

"You little shit," Holly said.

My whole body shook. "That's not funny," I yelled.

He waved his hand toward his face. "How about a little kiss to make me feel better?"

"Um, no, you can't get a kiss. How about I beat your ass?" I stumbled, trying to reach him. Holly grabbed my arm and held me back.

"Where's your mother?" Holly asked.

"Yeah, where is your mother? She should be here watching you," I yelled.

"I'm twelve years old. I don't need my mother watching over me," he sassed back, walking away.

"Oh yes you do. You still need a mother to watch over you," I shouted back.

"You okay, girl?" Holly asked.

"Yeah. Can you believe that kid? He pretended that his foot was stuck, and it wasn't. What a little jerk." I turned to find my rock. *Where is my geode?* "Holly, do you see my rock? It was right here!" I looked behind the boulder. It was gone. A boy a few feet away had it in his hands. "Can I have that rock?" I yelled over to him.

"Yeah, sure." He reached his hands out and then dropped it. The rock hit the side of the boulder and fell into the water. *Oh my God.*

I jumped back in the rushing water and ducked underneath. I could see Holly looking down in the water and saying, "Let it go, Sandy."

I came to the surface. "No. I almost had it. It was a geode. I know it was."

"It's gone. Let it go," Holly said again.

I plunged back into the water. When I opened my eyes, several tadpoles had circled me. They scattered when I moved my hands. There were a million rocks at the bottom of the river, and they all looked the same. I came up for air. "I can't find it," I yelled. "It's gone. I can't believe it I...I had it in my hands, and then he...he fell, and all I did was try and save him, and now it's gone." I slapped the water. "I'm so mad right now!" I slapped and punched the water several more times.

"Come on. There's nothing we can do right now. Do you need help getting out?"

"No. I'm—I'm fine." I climbed out of the water, scraping my knee in the process. *Great, now I'll probably have a scar for the rest of my life.*

"Let's go back to camp and get something to eat. Aren't you hungry? I'm starving," Holly said.

My body shivered, and my heart raced. "I'm not hungry. But, I'm ready to go back."

We started back down the trail. "Tell me again why you need to find a geode?"

"Because I—I lost the one thing that I was hoping to find on this trip."

"I know. But, you could have drowned trying to find that stupid rock."

"It's not a stupid rock, and no, I wouldn't have drowned. All I had to do is stand up. The water wasn't that deep. Besides, I'm a Cactus Girl. Nothing is going to hurt me."

Further down the trail, Holly picked up a pine cone. "Can you believe the size of these pine cones? They're the size of your head." She held it out to me. "How about a giant pine cone instead? I'm sure there's something inside."

"Very funny." I took it from her and threw it back into the woods.

"Oh no, that was my favorite pine cone," Holly said, laughing.

I covered my face with my hands. "I'm sorry. I guess I'm overreacting. It's just a rock."

Holly bumped my shoulder. "Ah, don't be sorry. I love it when you get mad. It's good for you to let it out. And besides, I would have loved to see you kick that boy's ass."

My mouth tensed. *It's not over yet. I'm still going to get my geode.*

Before we got to our campground, we walked over to see Bridalveil Falls. The water cascaded down from high above and then draped outward at the bottom, resembling a long bridal veil. "It looks like we got to Yosemite at the right time. The Yosemite newspaper said by the end of June, no water would flow over the falls. But, they had a significant snowpack last winter, and the water was still flowing like crazy."

We cleaned up at our campsite, changed into dry clothes, and headed to the Curry Village Pizza Deck. We ordered a pizza and Diet Cokes and sat outside on the deck. Just as I took my last bite of pizza, a man who looked in his fifties and wearing a brown apron stood at our table.

"Can I get you young ladies anything else?"

"Ah, no, we're fine," Holly said.

He picked up our empty pizza box. "How long will you be staying at the park?"

"Just one more day," I added.

"Robert, you're wanted in the kitchen." A girl who looked a few years older than me tapped him on his shoulder.

"I'm on my way. Maybe we'll meet again," he said, walking away.

"I see you met Robert," the girl continued.

"Kinda," I said.

"My name is Magdalena. Mind if I join you?" She sat across from me.

"No. I guess not. I'm Holly, and this is Sandy."

"Robert is my boyfriend. And I guess I should tell you he's the father of my son, who's three."

I glanced at Holly and raised my eyebrows.

Holly swirled the straw in her Coke. "Um, we were just eating when he came up to us."

"Oh, I know. Robert is a big flirt. He can't help flirting with pretty young girls."

"Well, you don't need to worry about us. We're not interested," I said.

"How old are you?" Holly asked.

"I'm twenty-four. I know Robert is way older, but I love him."

"Do you work here too?" I asked.

"Yes. I came here to work four years ago. The hospitality school I was going to required us to work at various National Parks to get experience."

"What do you do?" Holly asked.

"I run the daycare for the workers. And then I met Robert, fell in love, and never left. I didn't want to leave anyway because of my son. I want him to be with his father."

"So, you live here year-round?" Holly asked.

Magdalena shifted. "Yes, I love it here. I wouldn't want to be anywhere else. And after Robert met me, he decided to stay too." She cocked her head. "Sometimes, you have to follow your heart. Oh, wait one minute." Magdalena hurried over to a table next to us, picked up a few dollars left for a tip, and then walked back to our table.

"Did you just steal that money?" Holly asked.

Magdalena shrugged. "It's not stealing if you find it. Besides, stealing makes me feel like...I'm in control, you know, like I have power."

It does?

165

"Does Robert know you steal his tips?" Holly asked.

Magdalena smirked. "What's his…is mine. Do you know what the name Magdalena means in the Bible?"

We both shook our heads.

"It means 'Watchtower.' I am a Watchtower. I watch over everything, including Robert. Besides, Robert doesn't need to know. He's supposed to be paying child support for his son, and he doesn't, so I take what I can get."

I think it means you're crazy.

"Why do you stay with him if he doesn't support you and his son? Doesn't that hurt you, that he doesn't care?" Holly asked.

"I stay because he's mine."

He's yours? What does that mean? I stood. "Well, we're the Cactus Girls. Are you ready to go, Holly?"

"Yep. I'm done here."

"Cactus Girls?"

"Yeah. Do you know what that means?"

Magdalena's eyes squinted and she shook her head.

I pulled my shoulders back. "Cactus Girls don't allow people to steal from us or hurt us."

We walked down the steps toward the campground. Magdalena followed and shouted out. "One day, you'll have a story of what you've overcome and gone through, and you'll tell everyone."

I turned to face her. "Yep, and it will become someone else's survival guide." *What a crazy girl. I don't ever want to be like Magdalena. Stealing from one person because another person wronged you isn't right. I guess learning from others will be my survival story.*

On the way back to the campground, Holly and I walked along the river. We stopped and skipped stones across the water. A couple of young boys no more than ten years old were casting fishing poles in the babbling water. Holly stopped. "I think I'm ready to head home tomorrow. How about you?"

"Yeah. I guess I'm ready too." Neither one of us spoke for a few minutes. "After all these weeks, I'm really bummed I haven't found a geode."

"Maybe that rock you found in the falls was a geode. But then you lost it."

"Well, if that was one, there should be more, don't you think?"

"Gray guy told you that you could find them in river beds, right?"

"Yeah."

"Maybe one of these rocks is a geode." Holly pointed into the water rushing along the side of the river. "Why don't you grab one."

I looked up and down the river and brushed some tall grass away from an almost round rock. I lifted the gray rock out of the ground and washed the mud off in the flowing water, holding on tight, so I wouldn't lose it. "What do you think? Geode or not?"

"Maybe if you want to believe it's a geode, it will be. To me, it's a rock."

Maybe Holly's right, it's just a rock. But I can still hope it's a geode.

Back at the campsite, Holly and I sat at the picnic bench. I placed my rock on top and spun it around. I searched for a hairline fracture. *Geode or not, at least I have a souvenir to take home and a couple of stories of what I went through to get it.*

I grabbed my rock and set it next to the tent as I crawled inside.

A few minutes later, a man approached our tent. "Do you mind if I borrow your rock?"

I backed out of the tent. A man about in his late twenties was standing next to Holly.

"One of the stakes on my tent broke." He pointed over to his campsite, where one side of his tent was lying on the ground. A woman around the same age waved. "Would you mind if I use it to hold the rope down?"

I closed my eyes. *You can't be serious. Do you know how long it took me to find this? How many days, weeks? I risked my life to find a geode, and now you think I should just give this to you?* I glanced at Holly. She shrugged her shoulders.

"Yeah, sure, I guess," I said quietly.

"We just need it for one more night," he said.

"Okay. I was hoping to take it home as a souvenir."

"I'll give it back to you in the morning. I promise."

I took a deep breath. "All right."

He bent down and picked it up. "I'll leave it on the picnic table in the morning." He turned and walked back to his campsite. "Thanks again. Have a nice night."

My geode was being carried away in the arms of a strange man. "Yeah, you too."

The man pulled his tent upright and tied the rope around my rock. That was where my geode was going to spend the night.

The following day, Holly, and I both woke up with the sun peeking in through the unzipped flap of our tent. Holly nudged me. "I say we get packed and head home."

I agreed. *Oh yeah, my rock.* I scrambled out of my sleeping bag, and pushed open the flaps.

"Holly! Holly."

"What?"

"They're gone!" I ran to the picnic table. My rock wasn't there. Holly joined me outside. "They just left and took my rock with them."

"Are you sure? Let's go over and look for it."

I pointed at the ground where the man's tent was. "It was right here, and now it's gone. They took it. They took my geode."

Holly kicked some dirt around where their tent was. "Why would they want that stupid rock?"

"It's not a stupid rock. It was a geode. I know it."

"I meant how would they know it was a geode. To them, it was just a rock. Maybe they needed it for their tent where ever they were going next."

I scanned the campground. "Or maybe they knew it was a geode and wanted it for themselves."

Holly walked back to the tent and started taking it down.

"I shouldn't have trusted him. I'm never going to trust anyone ever again."

"I don't think he took it on purpose. You'll find another geode."

"No, I won't!" I kicked the ground. Dirt scattered. "We're leaving now! And I'll never have a chance to find another one." Holly handed me the tent poles. She rolled the tent up and we stuffed it in the canvas bag.

🚗🚗🚗

On the way out of the park, we passed several small fires burning in the woods. We learned later they were called prescribed burns, where firefighters start fires to destroy the brush that fire depends on. The land was then cleared for

169

regrowth of new plants and trees, restoring health to the ecosystem. *Maybe I should burn away everything lying around that does me no good and hope for something new. Hmm, but where would I start?*

I mapped out the route to Breckenridge. "We can either go the northern route through Salt Lake City or the southern route through Las Vegas. Which one?"

"Southern route," Holly said with a giant smile on her face.

I figured she'd say that. Southern route it was. "Holly, pull into that gas station so I can call Karen."

"Do you think she'll answer this time?"

"Probably not, but at least she'll know I tried."

I dialed the same number I've been calling since I left. The phone rang five times, the answering machine picked up. "Hey, Karen, it's me again. Well, we're leaving Yosemite now. Um, where did I leave off last time? Oh yeah, LA. We drove north up the coast of California to San Jose. We stopped at The Mystery House, the Winchester House that the Smith and Wesson gun guy's daughter owned. It was pretty weird. The daughter of the gun guy kept building all these rooms that made no sense. She did it to ward off evil spirits from people who died from a Smith and Wesson gun. I hope I don't get crazy in my old age. And then we drove into San Francisco. Wow, what a city. We rode around the city on a trolley. We drove down a few streets that were in movies and then past the Golden Gate Park and down Haight Ashbury Street. There were a lot of hippies and potheads playing guitars and singing made-up songs. I don't want a life like that. Then Holly and I drove across the Golden Gate Bridge. It was huge, so tall and beautiful and sort of sad too. Did you know they have nets under the bridge, to catch people if they jump off? Yosemite is so great. The granite rocks are massive.

The biggest one is El Capitan, and then Half Dome. I'm sure you've seen pictures. Did you know that people hike to the top of Half Dome on cables? Even though I'm a Cactus Girl, that was too scary for me.

"I think I might have found a geode in the water in Yosemite. I almost died trying to get it, but I couldn't reach it. I'll tell you the story when I get home. We've met so many friendly people on this trip, but this girl we met last night, her name is Magdalena. She's only a few years older than me, but she had a baby with a man who was way older than her, and she lives here, at the park. I don't think I could live in a park even though it's so awesome here. I've learned a lot out here, talking to people we meet and seeing how they live. In one of the gift shops here, there was a picture of Half Dome and the words that said "Climb a mountain, and even though it's hard—don't quit."

"I think I know what I want to do now. I want to go to beauty school. Do you think that would be good? I know I talked about going back to Chicago, but I don't think there's anything for me back home anymore. I'll keep thinking about it and let you know what I want to do when I get home. Holly keeps saying she wants to drive through Las Vegas on the way home, so we are going the southern route through Vegas. I think she's going to go to Vegas after she drops me off. I'm afraid that after she leaves, she'll change and I'll lose my best friend." I swallowed a few times. *What am I going to do without my best friend?* "I'm glad I live with you and Dan and Kelsey." I paused and brushed a tear away. "Well, I guess I better get off the phone. We'll probably stay over one more night and be home late tomorrow, so I won't be calling anymore. I'll be seeing you instead. Bye."

171

EIGHTEEN

Chasing Losses

We drove south through California, past Bakersfield, and northeast into Las Vegas. Seven hours later, we arrived in Sin City.

Even though it was still light out, flashing fluorescent lights lit up the sky everywhere I looked. We drove down the main strip. Hundreds of people were walking on the sidewalks and overhead bridges that spanned between buildings. Buildings shaped like a colorful hot air balloon, an Eiffel Tower, a tall flat, reflective gold building where the sunshine bounced off nearly blinding you, a black and gold pyramid shaped structure, a stratosphere building, and a castle in the sky sprawled along the famous strip. In front of one hotel, hundreds of dancing streams of water shot several hundred feet in the air, swaying to music and lights against a lavender sky. Billboards high in the sky showcased tigers on gold leashes, magician shows, and "Get married by Elvis" flashing in red and black lights. *Isn't he dead?*

Holly parked the car in an upper parking garage and elbowed me. "What do you think?"

"This is crazy. All these people and...and everything. I could watch the dancing water for hours. It was so pretty.

This is so different than I dreamed Vegas would be like. It feels like a fantasy here."

"I know, right? I love this. It's like being high without getting high—in a good way. Let's go walk around and check out some of the casinos."

"Can we get in?"

"Yeah, I think. But let's try anyway. What do we have to lose?"

Walking from the parking garage to the strip, a couple of girls dressed in skimpy outfits barely covering their private parts handed us cards with more nearly naked girls on them and a phone number to call. Holly and I both immediately dropped the cards. Taxis and buses drove by, advertising more half-naked women and topless men for sale. 'Just call the flashing phone number, and they will be at your door.'

Around the corner, the Manhattan skyline stood in front of us. We stopped directly in front of the Empire State Building with a full-sized Statue of Liberty in front.

"Is that a roller coaster?"

Seconds later, the roar of the coaster rushing down the rails soon turned to screams as it looped around and then turned into a corkscrew. I pointed at the New York New York casino in front of us. "This one. Let's go in here."

Holly grabbed my arm. "Okay, now when we walk in, pretend like you own the place. Maybe security won't notice us."

We pushed open the double glass doors and followed the people walking toward the casino floor. At the entrance, a man and woman were arguing loudly. When the woman pushed and slapped the man, two security guards standing near them grabbed them by their arms and walked them out of the casino. Holly and I slid inside behind them.

The minute we stepped on the dark-red carpet, the scent of gardenia hit my nose. Then, a mix of chaotic flashing neon lights. A musical scale of ringing bells and sirens rang out. Sounds of coins hitting metal and spinning wheels lit up the room—gamblers were casually dressed, jackets on the back of their chairs sitting at tables playing poker.

"Do you hear that, Sandy? All those bells ringing, someone must be winning."

It sounds like a lot of people are winning. We need to be winning. I want to win someday. "Are you sure we can play and not get in trouble?"

"I don't see why we can't play," Holly said.

We walked past tables where red dice rolled down green carpets and a small white ball rolled inside a spinning wheel, then down isles of one cent and twenty-five cent slot machines. Lights strobed on and off. A voice echoed from a slot machine. "Try your luck. You might get rich, but not if you don't play."

"Which one should we play?" Holly asked.

I scanned the row in front of us. One was a poker game. *I have no idea how to play poker. The last time I played poker with my friends, I lost my shirt.* "No, not this one." At the next machine, you had to match cherries and oranges. *I can't eat oranges. They bother my stomach.* "No, not this one either." The next game caught my eye. A black cat wearing a witch's hat meowed and hopped onto a ladder. "This one, Holly. There's a cat on it. It's called Hex Breaker. It says, "Change your luck."

Holly looked around the casino. My eyes followed. Cocktail servers wearing gold satin bustiers and short black satin skirts with fishnet stockings shuffled by carrying drinks. "Nice, Holly. I love their uniforms."

175

"Yeah." Holly smiled. "I think I could work here." After Holly watched the waitress sashay across the room, she pulled out a dollar bill, fed the machine, and sat down on the leather chair. I stood next to her. Lights flashed, and Hoodoo, the cat, screeched. We both nervously scanned the area again. "What do I do?" Holly asked.

"Pull the lever."

Holly pulled the lever toward her. The lever ticked like she was pulling a big crank. "Let the fun begin." Lights flashed again, and the three rows and five columns with icons of black cat faces, the number 13, a shoe stepping on a crack, broken hand mirrors, open umbrellas, and a face of a black raven, a copper penny, the word hex breaker, and step ladders randomly flickered across the columns. My heart raced with every spin. When the columns stopped spinning, there were no matches.

"Pull it again, Holly."

Holly pulled the lever two more times. No matches, and our money was gone. I yanked a dollar bill from my front pocket, slid into the chair, and fed the slot. I pulled the lever. The columns spun. No matches. A lump rose in my throat. I pulled the lever again. "Come on, come on. Land on something." No matches again. I had one more spin left. I closed my eyes and silently said a prayer, *God, please make them all match…please, please. Okay, maybe just a few, make a few match. All right, just one, how about one match.* I pulled the lever. My heart pounded. I opened my eyes and held my breath. Four broken hand mirrors lined up. "Holly, Holly, we got a bonus spin." Hoodoo, the cat, screeched and appeared on the screen. I rubbed the screen. "Shhhhh." *Not so loud, kitty.*

The screen faded, and then fourteen different-sized and shaped mirrors popped up. The lights around the mirrors flashed "Pick five mirrors. Try your luck. HAHAHA."

I peered over my shoulder. "Holly, is anyone watching?"

Holly scanned to room. "No, I don't see anyone."

"Keep an eye out."

"I am, I am."

"If anyone looks at you, don't make eye contact."

My stomach fluttered. *Which one should I pick?* I chose the round mirror in the far-right corner. The mirror popped, a lightning bolt flashed across the screen, and broken pieces scattered. $75 lit up. "Holly, we made seventy-five dollars." Next, I picked the long, rectangular mirror. $100.00. Another lightning bolt cracked, and broken mirror pieces fell.

"Shhhhh."

"Okay, okay." I stepped to the side. "You pick two."

Holly picked the oval mirror in the middle. Broken pieces revealed $50.00, then the square mirror next to it flashed $25.00.

"Nice, Holly." I took my time selecting the last mirror. Finally, I hit the small rectangular mirror next to the one Holly chose. $200.00. My mouth fell open. I grabbed Holly's arm. "Holly, we won seventy-five…a hundred…two hundred…fifty and twenty-five. Ah that's four hundred fifty dollars."

The mirrors disappeared and the columns were back. Holly stepped in and pulled the lever. All the rows spun and spun. "Keep going. We need a jackpot." No matches. She pulled the lever again. Nothing matched again on the second, third, or fourth pulls. After a few more spins, our four fifty went down to three fifty. My stomach turned. "Holly, we're losing our money."

"I can see that." She rubbed her hands on her shorts. "Don't worry. We'll get it back."

"Okay. But when we get back to four hundred, we're going to stop and cash out."

"Okay, okay." She pulled several more times, and each time I scanned the room looking for security or anyone watching us. Our winnings went down to two hundred.

I swallowed hard. *We're losing all our money.* "Let me try again." After three more spins, we gained forty dollars, and then on the next spin, we lost it. I pulled one more time. Four step ladders matched. *Finally.* The screen faded out, and a yellow step ladder with twelve steps on each side popped on the screen.

"What's happening now?" Holly asked.

"I don't know, but a black raven is on top of the ladder and Hoodoo is in the corner licking his paw." The game said to touch the Fortune board. The bonus round will be over if you land on the top step where the black crow sits or on a previous landed step. So, I touched the Fortune board. The number 10 lit up.

Hoodoo bounced from step to step and stopped on the tenth step. $125.00 lit up. The word CROW was highlighted on the step. *Yes.* I pressed the board again. *Don't land on the CROW step Hoodoo.* The cat hopped up eight more steps. $300.00 lit up, and the step lit up with CROW. I screamed inside. "Come on, Hoodoo. Make us rich." The third time Hoodoo hopped up thirteen steps. $225.00 lit up. The word CROW lit up that step. I looked down at the credits. "Oh my God, Holly, we're up to eight hundred fifty." *If Holly and I split it, I'll have four hundred and twenty-five dollars. I could totally buy new clothes and a new pair of tennis shoes; I could buy anything I wanted. Maybe my luck is changing.* My hands were shaking when I

178

touched the board. Hoodoo bounced up four steps and landed on the step I previously landed on that was lit up with CROW. The game said "Time to eat crow, HAHAHA" and the bonus round was over. The ladder faded out. *Darn it.* The columns and rows were back.

"My turn," Holly said.

I touched her hand. "I think we should stop."

"No. Our luck has changed. A few more minutes, then we'll quit." Holly pulled the lever over and over. There were no matches and our winnings went down to four hundred.

"Holly, stop. We're losing all our money."

"All right. You try. You had better luck. Try and get us back to at least five hundred, then we'll quit for sure."

I sat down. "Okay, but that's it. Five hundred, and then we quit."

I pulled the lever. The columns scrolled by. No hits. *Damn it.* I pulled the lever again. No matches. I increased my bet, still nothing matched up. My hands were sweating. Our money was disappearing with every pull.

We were down to two hundred. "This isn't working, Holly."

"Okay, try and get back to three hundred."

"I'm trying to get Hoodoo back." I pulled the lever eight more times. We were down to one twenty. I wanted to keep going, but our money was disappearing. *Why aren't we winning anymore?* I stopped. *How can this be? We were up eight fifty and now...* "That's it. We're cashing in."

"But we only have a hundred and twenty dollars. I want our money back. I'm so bummed right now."

"I know. Me too. This game must be rigged." I pressed the cash-out button. A ticket shot out. "Let's go get our money. At least we can buy something good to eat."

We followed the overhead signs for the cashier's station. "Holly, look at the sign above the cashier."

'You must be 21 with proof of ID.'

"Crap. What are we going to do now?"

"I don't know. We need to walk away."

We started walking. I glanced behind me. "Do you think anyone was watching us? I feel like someone is watching us."

"No. I think we're good. But if someone looks at us, just smile."

I looked around the room again. "Holly, look up."

Holly slowly glanced up. "Are those cameras?"

"I think so. Someone's probably been watching us the whole time."

"What if we get caught? Do you think they'll throw us in jail?"

"I don't know, and I sure don't want to find out."

"Let's go in the bathroom and figure out what to do."

We waited until the bathroom was empty. Holly pulled the ticket out of her pocket. "If we can't cash it in, what's the point? I'm not going to risk going to jail."

I grabbed the ticket. "Neither am I, but I'm not throwing this money away. I worked hard for this money."

Holly laughed and pulled the ticket from my hand. "And so did I." We both laughed.

Holly grabbed my hand. "You hold on to the ticket, and let's go walk around and see if we can find another way to get our money."

We peeked around the corner of the bathroom, looking for anyone who might be a security guard. "I think the coast is clear," Holly said. We tip-toed out, and a few feet away from the door, a skinny man wearing baggy blue cargo shorts, a white shirt, and a baseball cap waved at us.

I turned to see if anyone was behind us. "Holly, I think he's waving at us."

He waved again and took a few steps toward us.

"Oh, shit, Holly, he's coming to arrest us."

"This is it. We're going to jail."

My stomach sank. *I think I'm going to be sick.* "But I don't want to go to jail," I whispered.

Holly grabbed my arm. "Quick, let's go find another exit."

We quickly turned and walked toward the exit on the other side of the casino, zigzagging through the rows of slot machines and ducking around the cocktail waitresses and this time ignoring all the bells and sirens. *I hate those damn bells.* We were almost to the exit. We stopped and peered back. "I think we lost him," Holly said.

Please be gone. Please be gone. My life can't be over just because I wanted to win some money and buy a new pair of jeans and shoes.

We circled back and headed for the first exit where we came in. At the end of the row of slot machines, the man appeared in front of us.

Oh my God, how the hell did he find us?

"Girls, girls, girls. I'm thinking that you might have a little problem. Don't you?"

"Um, what do you mean?" Holly asked.

"I saw you by the cashier, and then you walked away. Do you have a ticket you can't cash?"

I took a step back. "Are you a security guard or the police? Because if you are, I think you're supposed to tell us."

"Yeah, you're supposed to tell us...we have rights."

The man laughed and shook his head. "No. No, I'm not security or the police." He stepped toward us and lowered his voice. "I can help you cash that ticket if you'd like."

Holly and I glanced at each other and then back at the man.

"How are you going to help?" Holly asked.

The man leaned in. "Keep your voice down."

Holly and I stepped back again.

"I can tell neither of you are old enough to gamble, and if you get caught, you'll both go to jail and be banned from ever stepping into any casinos again, for life."

Jail? Banned for life?

"Here's what I can do for you. I can cash that ticket in for a very small fee."

Holly stepped closer to him. "How much of a small fee?"

He motioned for the ticket. "How much did you win?"

I pulled the ticket out of my back pocket and held it up. "We won one hundred and twenty. We were up to eight hundred and fifty, but then we...we lost it."

The man chuckled. "Welcome to Vegas. I'll cash it in for you, and I'll only keep twenty. You'll get the rest."

"How can we trust you?" Holly asked.

Oh my God, yes, how? "Yeah, what if you take everything and run?"

He grinned. "What choice do you have? Don't cash it in and get nothing, or if you get caught, go to jail. Is that what you want?"

"No," We both said.

Holly and I looked around to see if anyone was watching. "Give him the ticket."

I held it out to her. "Are you sure?"

"Yeah. I guess. What else can we do?"

Holly handed him the ticket.

"Wait for me by Greenberg's Deli in the food court out past the casino. I'll be back in ten minutes."

I grabbed his arm. "Please don't run off with our money. This is all we have."

He pointed in the direction of the food court. "I'll be out there."

Twenty minutes later or maybe longer, Holly was sitting at a table outside Greenberg's Deli, holding her head in her hands.

I was pacing. "He's not coming back. I know it."

"Maybe there's a long line," Holly said.

I paced some more.

"Or maybe he got caught, and they arrested him. Or he ran off with our money," Holly added.

"Yeah, they should arrest him for stealing our money. Better him than us. Ugh. Why did we give him our ticket? He's probably a scam artist."

"I'll tell you who the scam artist is, the casino. They stole our money."

Yeah, they stole money we never had.

Every time someone walked into the food court, we jumped.

I sat for a few moments, and while I waited, I counted the number of people who walked in and out of Greenberg's Deli. I was up to twenty people. Their food looked so good. My stomach started growling. *What's taking so long?*

"He's here," Holly said.

I looked up. *Oh, my God.* "Finally."

Holly and I hurried toward him.

He held his hand up. "Slow down. I'm sorry it took so long. I had to make sure nobody was following me." His breath reeked of beer. He held out a hand to each of us. "Here's your cut."

I took the money from his right hand. "There's only forty here."

Holly counted her money. "I only got forty too. What gives?"

"I told you I had to get my cut."

"Yeah, but you said twenty. We should each get fifty and you twenty."

He backed away and raised his hands. "This is it. I gotta get going. Nice doing business with you. Oh, and by the way, next time, don't chase your losses." He scurried away before we could even say another word.

He just screwed us. We both stood in silence. I took a deep breath. *This is the worst day of my life.* "Holly?"

"Yeah?"

"I hate Las Vegas."

"I hear ya. Let's go eat and spend the money we have left before we lose it again."

I'm never going to tell anyone about this. Maybe it is true what people say about Vegas—What happens in Vegas stays in Vegas.

Holly and I split a corned beef sandwich piled four inches high on marble bread with yellow mustard and chips at Greenberg's Deli, and then walked down Las Vegas Boulevard and found the M&M Store. We each bought a large bag of plain M&M's. After that, we ate a stopped at a tee shirt shop and bought Las Vegas tee shirts. After shopping, Holly and I each had five dollars and eighty-five cents left. We took the long way back to the car, passing the MGM Grand, The Tropicana, and the Excalibur Hotels and Casinos. The billboards and lights weren't flashing as bright as they were before.

"So, what do you think?" Holly asked.

"Think about what?"

"Living here."

"Ah, I don't know. But do you really think you could live here? And where would you work?"

"You could work anywhere. Look how many places are here. I think it would be fun."

I stopped and faced her. "So, this is where you want to be?"

Holly walked past me and then stopped and turned. "Yeah…I do."

My stomach sank.

NINETEEN

Someone Saved My Life Tonight

We left the Vegas strip, drove a few more hours, and found a cheap hotel in St. George, Utah. I hardly slept that night, thinking about Holly wanting to move to Vegas.

In the morning, with only seven more hours to Breckenridge, we stopped at McDonald's for breakfast and then a gas station to fill up. I emptied the cooler, tossed our garbage in the trash can, and leaned against the car, waiting for Holly to finish. *Vegas is where Holly wants to be, and I can't change that. I thought I was the only one who needed to figure out what to do after high school. I guess she did too, and it looks like she beat me to it. I need to be Cactus Girl strong. Maybe she'll change her mind.* A dog barking across the street grabbed my attention.

Near a boarded-up restaurant with a six-foot chain-link fence enclosing it, a man wearing a dirty white wife-beater tank top was tying a dog with a rope around his neck to a chain-link fence.

I walked toward the road. "Holly."

Holly looked up from pumping gas. "What?"

I pointed across the street. "What do you think is going on over there?"

187

We both watched. "What's that guy doing? Is he tying that dog to the fence?"

"Yeah. That's what it looks like."

Holly finished pumping gas and moved next to me. The man quickly walked back to his white, dented pickup truck and reached into the back of the truck. He carried a bag that looked like dog food, shuffled over near the dog, and sprinkled food on the ground.

"What's he doing now?"

"I don't know."

The dog jumped at the man, and he shoved the dog away. He leaned the bag against the fence. The dog sniffed the bag of food and then ran toward the man, who rushed back to his truck. The rope pulled on the dog's neck and snapped him back. The dog barked and squirmed, shaking its head. Dirt and stones sprayed the dog as the truck sped onto the desolate road. I took a few more steps closer. "Oh my God, I think he just left him."

Holly followed me. "No way. He better not have left that dog here."

"I think he did, Holly." The truck disappeared down the road. My heart sank as it drove further down the road. *Maybe he'll turn around and come back and get him. You can't just leave and abandon people... I mean animals like that.* My heart ached. I took a deep breath and held back my tears. *I'm a Cactus Girl. I'll be strong for you.*

Holly and I ran across the road to the dog when the truck was out of sight. The whitish blue-gray dog stopped barking when we approached it. I knelt in front of him and held my hand out. The dog slowly hopped closer to me.

"Why is he hopping?" Holly asked.

"I think he might be hurt." I reached over and caressed his pointy, black ears. The dog hopped closer. He sniffed and licked my hand. "Holly, can you tell if it's a girl or boy?"

"Hey, buddy, are you okay?" Holly bent down and peeked underneath. "It's a boy."

The dog lifted his right paw. Then, when I touched his foot, he pulled it back. "It's okay. I'm not going to hurt you." *And I'm not going to let you be abandoned on the side of the road either.*

Holly brushed his short fur and scratched his head. "What should we do? We can't leave him here."

The dog tugged on the rope as he tried to get closer to us. "Holly, go get the knife Kai gave us. It's in the glove box."

Holly ran across the road, drove the car over, and parked next to us. "Here's the knife," she said, stepping out of the car.

"Hold him while I cut the rope." I held my foot down on the rope, held the other end tight, and ran the sharp blade across the rope several times until one end fell. "Okay, I got it. He's free." The rope swung back and forth when he shook his head. The dog hopped over to Holly and me and held his right leg up. "He's hurt, Holly. I think we need to take him to a vet or a shelter or somewhere."

Holly and I lifted him into the back seat and put his bag of dog food in the trunk. I slid in next to him. We drove back to the gas station and asked where the nearest veterinary hospital was.

"There's one a few miles down the road," the gas station attendant said.

A few minutes later, we pulled into Dr. Anne's Veterinary Clinic. Inside, a young woman was at the counter. "How can I help you?"

189

Holly helped me carry the dog in. I stepped up to the counter. "Are you a doctor?"

"No. I'm a technician. How can I help you?"

"Um, we found this dog tied to a fence, and I think he's hurt."

"He won't let us touch his paw either," Holly said.

"Oh no." The technician walked around the counter. "Let's see where the problem is."

I called the dog over to me so she could see him limping.

"Yep, it looks like something is going on with the right foot." She raised his right paw and brushed her fingers over the pad on his foot. He yelped and pulled his paw back quickly. "I think he has glass or something sharp inside. Let's take him in the exam room and have the doctor look at him." Holly and I carried him in the exam room, lifted him onto the table, and then sat across from him. The technician filled a metal pan with water and soap and washed his paw. Dirt and dried blood mixed in the water. Blood dripped from the wound. "It looks like there's a large piece of glass in his foot. I'll have Dr. Anne look at him."

A few minutes later, the door opened. "Hello, I'm Dr. Anne." Holly and I both said hi. "How long has he been limping?"

"We don't know. We just found him today."

"So, he's not your dog?"

"No. Some guy dropped him off and tied him to a fence and then left a bag of dog food next to him," Holly said.

"Do you know what kind of dog he is?"

Dr. Anne lifted his chin. "He looks like an Australian Cattle dog. Sometimes they're called Blue Heelers."

"How big will he get?" I asked.

"Cattle dogs can get up to twenty inches tall and thirty-five to fifty pounds."

At least he won't be a big dog.

"Now, let's see what's causing him so much pain." She ran her fingers over his paw and then used a magnifying glass. "There's definitely glass or something sharp in there." She turned to the technician. "Let's muzzle him so he won't bite." The doctor and the technician held him down, sliding a black metal and leather harness over his face as he tried to back away. My heart pounded. *Oh, my God. Please don't hurt him.* Blood continued to drip from his paw as he struggled under their weight. "Do you really need to muzzle him?" *Children shouldn't be muzzled.* "Children are to be seen and not heard" echoed in my head. *No! No! Children are to be seen and heard.* My mother didn't need a black metal muzzle. She muzzled me with her words. I closed my eyes and took a deep breath.

"It'll be okay. We have to use a muzzle so he doesn't bite. He doesn't understand that we're trying to help him," the technician said.

"Hand me the alligator forceps," the doctor ordered. The technician opened the drawer and handed her a metal tool with metal teeth on the end. Dr. Anne slid her fingers into the holes. The teeth of the clamp closed. The doctor fished out a piece of glass about the size of a large paper clip from his foot. More blood dripped from the wound. The dog whimpered but laid still. "It looks like we got all the glass out." The technician washed his paw again and poured an orange liquid over it. Iodine. *Ouch. Poor dog.* Dr. Anne left the room, and the technician wrapped pads and gauze around his foot. When she was done, it looked like he was wearing a boxing glove. A few minutes later, the doctor walked back, opened the cabinet, pulled a vial from the shelf, inserted a

191

needle into it, and drew out the liquid. The dog lifted his head. Our eyes met. "Ready to hold him again?"

"Ready," the technician answered.

Dr. Anne held the scruff of his neck and injected the needle. The dog squirmed and moaned through the muzzle. "I'm going to finish my exam and make sure everything else is okay." After the exam, the doctor removed the muzzle, checked his eyes, lifted his lip and gums, and ran her hands along his belly. The technician lifted him off the table and left the room. The dog limped over to Holly and me and sat between us. I reached down and scratched his head.

"Other than this cut on his foot, he looks pretty good," Dr. Anne said.

"How much do you charge for this?"

"The removal of the glass, cleaning the wound, bandage, and antibiotics is about two hundred. You said you found him?"

Holly and I both nodded.

"Okay, then I'll keep him here until Animal Control comes to get him."

"What will happen to him then?" I asked.

"I'll call Animal Control when you leave. They will pick him up today or tomorrow if they aren't busy. If they can't find the owner, they'll take him to the animal shelter, and if nobody adopts him, then he most likely will be put down."

The dog whimpered and lowered himself on the cold tile floor, resting his head on his outstretched legs. My heart dropped. *No! No! Nobody is going to put him down or take him from me.* I knelt next to him and brushed his fur. "Why would they have to put him down? He seems like a nice dog."

"Unfortunately, there's too many dogs in the shelters and not enough good people to give them good homes."

"Can't we take him?" I asked.

"I can't make that decision. If the dog is a stray, I have to turn him over to Animal Control. You would have to adopt him from the animal shelter where they take him to, and your parents would have to approve the adoption. The shelter will make sure the dog goes to a good home." Dr. Anne pulled an orange pill bottle from the pocket of her white coat. "But whoever takes him will have to give him one of these pills every day for seven days so the cut won't get infected." She placed the bottle on the counter.

She patted his head. "I'm going to go back to my office and call Animal Control. You can say goodbye to the dog and see your way out the front. Thanks for bringing him in." The doctor walked out and closed the door behind her.

I brushed the dog's face and rubbed his ears. A tear escaped from both the dog's eyes and mine. I brushed our tears away. "Holly, I can't let him go to Animal Control. We can't leave him here to die."

She pulled me up. "Yes, I know, but what are we going to do with him?"

"I'll take him. You heard the doctor. They're going to kill him."

Holly rubbed his head, and he licked her hand. "All right, I agree. We can't leave him here. So, what's our plan then?"

I looked through the window of the door the doctor walked out of. I didn't see anyone. "Um, we'll sneak him out the front door. You go first in case someone is out front." Holly opened the door and peeked around the corner. She waved for me to come. I grabbed the rope, and we lifted him and carried him out the front door. Before I closed the door, I grabbed the bottle of antibiotics off the counter and shoved it in my pocket. We put him in the back seat and then jumped

193

in front. "Wait, Holly," I said before she drove off. I opened the glove box and grabbed the money we hid inside. I counted out two hundred dollars and ran back into the clinic, tossed the money on the counter, and dashed out. *Kai told us to save a life with this money.*

I jumped back in the car and yelled. "Go, go." I looked back to see if anyone was running after us. I sunk down in the seat. "Oh, my God, Holly, did we just steal a dog?"

Holly laughed and nodded as she sped away like Thelma and Louise running from the police. "I think we did, but finders' keepers, right?"

A few miles down the road, no cops were speeding toward us. So, I figured we were safe.

Holly glanced in the rearview mirror. "Your dog needs a name."

I turned and watched him resting his head on the backseat. "What's your name?" He tilted his head. I studied the black-and-white face patches around his eyes that looked like he was wearing a mask. His dark eyes shifted with every sound. "I have to think about this for a minute." He needs to have a cool name. Something meaningful that will forever remind me of how he came into my life. Every dog's name came and went in my head. I looked over at Holly. "Oh, I know. How about Ranger?"

"Why Ranger?" Holly asked.

"That was the name on the truck of the guy who dumped him off. It was a Ford Ranger."

Holly shook her head. "No. You don't want to be reminded of the man who dumped him."

"Yeah, you're right." I turned to the back seat again. "How about…Kai? Yes. I think we should call him Kai. Because Kai gave us money and told us to save a life."

"Yes, I love it. And Kai gave us the knife too, which we used to cut him free. Or should we call him Benjamin?" Holly snickered.

I nodded. "I guess we should start calling Benjamin by his real name and the dog Kai from now on." I reached over the front seat and held his face. "How do you like your new name, Kai?" Kai licked my hand and barked.

Holly grinned in the rearview mirror. "I think he likes it."

"Yes, he does." My heart was full. "Let's go home."

We drove north on Highway 15, skirting around the Dixie National Forest and then east on Route I-70 through the Fishlake National Forest. Signs for the Arches National Forest in Moab, where our journey started, showed along the two-lane highway. Away from the small towns, out on the open road, more wild horses ran like the wind—kicking up their heels and dust across the grasslands, running wild and free. I watched them until the highway carried us further down the road to home. I no longer wanted to be a horse, running free. I just wanted to belong to someone.

I looked back at Kai, and a beautiful light sparkled in his dark brown eyes. He and I had been lost in the dark for so long. Now, we both were found and belonged to someone. I'm going to hang on to what I have. *I saved a life today.*

TWENTY

Your Journey is not Mine and My Journey is not Yours

At the exit sign to Breckenridge, I stuck my head out of the car's open window and breathed in the familiar fresh scent of pine trees that I had grown to love since moving to Colorado. Twenty minutes later, Holly parked in front of Karen and Dan's house. "Home sweet home."

I sat for a few minutes. "You're not going home, are you?"

Holly turned to face me. "No."

Silence.

"What's with that look?" Holly asked.

"So, you're going back to Las Vegas?"

"Yes. But I'll be closer to you there than Chicago. Or you can come with me."

"No. I need to stay here." *Why do I care so much that Holly is going to Vegas? Is it because she's able to move on—by herself before me?* "I've got plans." *I think.*

Holly leaned back against the car door. "So, what are your plans?"

"Um, ah, I'm going to go…. Karen thinks I should go to beauty school, and I thought about it before, but I didn't think I could afford it. She told me I could get a loan to pay for school and get a job. So, that's what I think I'm going to do."

"I can see you being a great hairstylist."

"What if I'm terrible and cut someone's hair wrong, or dye it purple...or cut their ear off?"

Holly laughed. "Stop worrying about failing. And besides hair grows, and maybe one day someone might want purple hair."

"What are you going to do in Vegas?"

"I'll look for a waitress job and go from there."

"And you're not afraid to go alone?"

"No. And you shouldn't be either."

Fine then, I don't need anyone! But she's right, though. I don't need her to hold my hand anymore. But I want the people who I care about to be around me. I don't want them to leave. I swallowed hard. *I can do this too. I've got Kai, and that's all I need.*

When my mother left me last January, I felt an overwhelming sense of sadness, even though she'd been left me long before that day. I just didn't know it until she was physically gone and not in the next room. And now my best friend was forging her own path without me. *Who am I going to jump off cliffs, kill spiders, and steal dogs with? I guess I have to say goodbye to the life I knew and loved. I may have to do things afraid and alone, but I'll be okay.* I opened the car door.

"I'll help you," Holly said.

"No, that's okay. I got it." I opened the trunk, grabbed my backpack, and then opened the back door and helped Kai out.

Holly stepped out of the car. "Well, this is it, girl."

We hugged. "Yep. This is it." *I'm going to be okay.*

Sometimes you meet a girl, and she becomes your best friend. No matter the distance, no matter the time since you last saw her, she was still your best friend forever. Forever, we would be the Cactus Girls.

I waved goodbye as she drove down the street and turned left, heading back to Highway 70 West.

I pushed the front door open with my foot and dropped my backpack on the floor. Kai followed me in. The news was playing loudly on the TV. "Karen? Dan? Anyone?" I turned the TV off.

"Hey, you're back," Karen said, rushing into the living room, smiling. "You look good, all nice and tan, but you look tired."

"Oh, I'm dead tired."

"It's a dog," Kelsey yelled, running up to Kai and me.

"Whose dog is that?" Karen asked.

"Um, it's…my…dog."

Karen's smile disappeared.

Kelsey kneeled on the floor and lifted Kai's bandaged paw. "Is he hurt? Why does he have a bandage on? What's his name?"

"His name is Kai. And yes, he hurt his paw."

"Where did you get him?" Kelsey asked.

I told Karen the story of how we found him and took him to the vet. I didn't tell her that we stole him or that I named him after a hitchhiking surfer.

"I don't think Dan will be too happy about this," Karen said.

"Mommy, can we keep him?"

"No. Not now, Kelsey. What are your plans for…for…?"

"Kai? I'll take care of him. He's a really good dog."

Karen crossed her arms across her chest. "Dogs are expensive. And they are a lot of work. And how are you going to take care of him?"

"Mommy, Mommy, can we keep him?" Kelsey squealed again.

"Kelsey. We'll talk about this when your dad gets home. Kelsey laid on the floor next to Kai, petting him. "Now, young lady, I thought you said you would call me and let me know how everything was going and that you were all right? But, instead, all I got is one postcard from you."

My mouth fell open. *What?* "I did call you, Karen. I called you several times, and I left a voicemail for you every time. Didn't you get any of them?"

"No. There were no messages. And I've been home almost every day." Karen walked into the kitchen. I followed. She searched the answering machine sitting on the counter. "See? There are no messages."

I stared at the answering machine. "I—I don't know why." I walked back into the front room, pulled a piece of paper out of my backpack's zipped pocket, and held it out to Karen. "Here's the number I called."

"Well, well, I know why I didn't get any calls. This isn't my number." She pointed at the wrinkled paper. "This is a three, not an eight."

"What? Oh no! Who was I calling, then?"

"I don't know, but I'm glad you were okay and made it home safe."

My mind raced. *Who was I leaving messages for?*

"How was your trip, other than rescuing an abandoned dog?"

Karen and I sat at the kitchen table, and I told her all the stories of every place we went and the people we met while Kelsey continued to play with Kai on the floor and then started to sing to him. But I couldn't help but wonder who I had been calling.

"So, did you have fun with Holly?"

"Yeah. It was fun—except."

Karen rested her hand on her chin. "Except, what?"

"She's not going back to Chicago. She was always talking about Las Vegas, and when we drove through there on the way home, she said she wanted to stay. So, when she dropped me off, she said she was driving back there."

"And why is that a problem?"

"I don't know. I guess I thought she'd go back home and...."

"And what, do the same thing she's been doing all her life? She needs to explore what's out in the world for her too."

"I guess I feel like she's pulling away from me."

"She's moving on, not pulling away from you." Karen patted the top of my hand. "And you need to move on too. Friends come and go. Las Vegas isn't that far away, and you can go visit her, and someday you might find each other again." She looked down at Kai and Kelsey lying near my feet. "And when you go, take Kai with you." She laughed.

I watched Kai being loved by Kelsey. Then Kelsey jumped to her feet. "Oh, I got something for you." She ran down the hallway.

"So, what did you decide about going to beauty school?" Karen asked.

I smiled. "I think I'll go."

"Good! I think that's the best choice." Karen walked over to a folder on the counter, pulled a brochure out, unfolded it, and pointed at a date in September. "We need to get you registered now."

"All right, I'll call tomorrow and find out what I need to do to register."

"Ask them about loans, and then we'll go look for an apartment for you, and then I think you should look for a job too. Somewhere close to school and wherever you're going to live."

"Yeah, okay."

"Sandy, I have something for you," Kelsey said sneaking up behind me.

I turned. "What do you have for me?"

Kelsey opened her hand.

"My lip gloss."

"Yes. And I took really good care of it too." Kelsey smiled and motioned me to come closer. She whispered in my ear. "And I used some too. Don't tell Mommy."

"I won't," I whispered back.

Kai limped over to the front window and barked when a car pulled into the driveway. Then the garage door opened, and Kai hopped over by the back door and barked again. "Kai, come over here." He looked at me, then barked again. "It's okay. It's only Dan." I stood up and pulled him near me. "Sit."

The door opened. "Hey, you're home," Dan said, walking in wearing workout shorts and a Summit High School tennis tee shirt.

Kai barked.

"Ah, what's going on here?" Dan asked.

My heart raced.

Kelsey ran to Dan and wrapped her arms around his legs. "It's a dog, Daddy," Kelsey squealed. "Can we keep him? Can we? Can we?"

Dan rubbed his head. "Karen, what's going on?"

"Come sit down, Dan," Karen said.

"Do I want to hear this?" Dan leaned over and kissed the top of my head. "I'm glad to have you back. How was your trip? And why is there a dog in my kitchen?"

I told Dan the same story I told Karen. "So, you went out to find yourself and rescued a dog."

"Yeah, sorta. I know I should have asked you first, but I thought you would be okay with it once you met him. He's a good dog. He was great in the car. The vet said they would put him to sleep if nobody claimed him. I couldn't let that happen."

Kelsey tugged on my shirt. "What does that mean, to put him to sleep?"

How the heck do I explain this. "It means—"

"We don't need to talk about that now, Sandy," Karen said.

Kelsey hugged Kai. "I love this doggie and his pointy ears. Daddy, did you see he's wearing a mask," she shrieked.

Dan pulled Kelsey off Kai and sat her on his lap. "He looks like an Australian Cattle dog."

"He is. At least that's what the vet said. She also said he's probably full-grown. So, he shouldn't get any bigger."

Kelsey placed her hands on the sides of Dan's face and looked him in the eyes. "Daddy, can we keep him?"

Dan ran his hand over his chin. "Kelsey…."

"Sandy, how are you going to take care of this dog? You'll barely have enough money to support yourself and pay for school," Karen asked.

"I—I, haven't thought about that yet. I'm going to walk Kai and then go to bed. I'm exhausted," I said.

"We'll talk about Kai tomorrow," Dan said.

After my walk, I crawled into bed with Kai. He circled several times until he settled at the end of the bed by my feet.

A few minutes later, Kai scooted next to me, nudging my arm. I wrapped my arms around him, resting my hand on his side. In the middle of the night, I woke to Kai shaking and whimpering. I sat up. "Kai? Are you having a nightmare?" I pulled him into my arms and whispered in his ear. "It's going to be okay, Kai. I know because I've been through the same thing." Tears streamed down my cheeks, overcome by the memories of my mother leaving me. So many nights I woke from nightmares too. Soon the room was filled with Kai's snoring. "Nobody's going to hurt you again."

Before the sun came up, Kai was licking my face. "What? Kai, stop. What do you want?" He pawed my face and then hopped off the bed and stood by the door. I rolled over. "You have to go potty?" Again, Kai scratched at the door. I kicked off my blankets and slid out of bed, pulling on a pair of sweatpants and tugging a sweatshirt over my head. I slipped my feet into slippers. "Let's go. But you need to learn to sleep later, Kai."

When we walked into the kitchen, Karen and Dan were sitting at the table holding steaming cups of coffee.

"Good morning," Karen said.

"Good morning," I said quietly.

Kai hopped over to Dan and nudged his leg. Dan reached down and rubbed his head. "Hey, big boy. You're up early."

"Yeah, I know. I'm going to take Kai out."

"When you get back, we are going to talk about Kai," Karen said.

I stepped outside and closed the door behind me. *Oh crap. Dan and Karen are going to make me get rid of him. I just know it. I finally found someone to belong to, and now I have to get rid of him. It isn't fair. I love Kai. Why can't I have something of my own to love and to love me back? Maybe we'll run away like Dorothy and Toto did in*

The Wizard of Oz. I sat on the front steps and watched Kai hop around and then roll in the grass. *Kai loves me. I know it. Well, if he doesn't love me yet, he will.* My mind continued to race. We walked around the block, and Kai stopped at every bush and tree, sniffing, and lifting his leg to mark his territory. "Do you really have to do that, Kai?" He turned his head and a flicker of irritation shone in his puppy dog eyes. Finally, we got back to the house. I sucked in my breath. "Come on, Kai, let's go back in." We stepped inside.

Dan was waiting for me on the couch. "Have a seat."

I stood next to Kai and held his leash tight. "I already know what you're going to say."

"Really?"

Karen sat next to Dan.

"Yes, you're going to tell me I have to get rid of Kai. That I shouldn't have brought a dog home without permission and, and I'm not responsible enough, and I can't afford to take care of him. But...but Kai needs a home, he needs to know that someone loves him and will take care of him, and...."

"Kind of like you?" Karen asked.

I blinked away tears that rushed to the front of my eyes. *Yeah, kind of like me.*

Dan walked over to me and rested his hand on my shoulder. "Calm down for a minute."

"I am, I am."

"Well, two of the three things you said are correct."

I shook my head. "Huh?"

"Karen told me you decided to go to beauty school and you'll be looking for a job. How are you going to take care of Kai? You're going to be going to class during the day, right?"

"Yeah."

"Then you'll probably have to work at night after school and on weekends, right?"

I nodded. "Yeah."

"How will you have time for Kai?"

Kai barked three times.

I shrugged my shoulders.

"A dog needs lots of attention, and it's expensive to take care of a dog."

Wait, he said I was right about two of the three. Does that mean...?

"So, Karen and I decided you can leave Kai here. We'll take care of him."

"And you can come to visit anytime," Karen jumped in.

My lips fell apart.

"And besides, Kelsey would be very disappointed if we took him away," Karen said.

I nodded. "Karen, when does class start again?"

"The next class starts in six weeks."

I knelt and held Kai. "So, I'll only have a few more weeks to be with Kai?"

"Sandy...."

I swallowed hard and blinked back a few more tears. "I know." I took a deep breath. "Thanks, Karen and Dan. I know you weren't planning on getting a dog, and then I bring one home without asking. Thank you for not making me take Kai to a shelter." Kai barked. "I know Kai will be happy here."

Dan laughed. "And so will Kelsey. You created a monster."

"And if Kelsey isn't happy, nobody's happy." Karen laughed.

The next day, Kai snuggled by my side on my bed while I filled out the forms for beauty school. After, I rolled over and grabbed the phone off the nightstand. I dialed the number I had been calling the last four weeks. The phone rang several times. A woman picked up. "Hello?"

"Um, hello, I think I've been calling this number and leaving messages, and I wanted to say I'm sorry if I bothered you."

"Oh my, is this Sandy?"

"Yeah. I meant to call someone else, and somehow I dialed an eight instead of a three."

"Sandy, I'm glad you called. The number you were calling and leaving messages on was my aunt's phone. She told me that she listened to all your messages about your trip and she really enjoyed hearing about your adventures. Sadly, my aunt passed away yesterday."

I gasped. "Oh. I'm sorry. Ah?" *What should I say?*

"Are you home from your trip?"

"Yes, I'm back in Breckenridge."

"Oh good. I'm in Breckenridge too. Would you be able to stop by sometime? My aunt left something for you."

"Ah, yeah, I can do that."

"Good. I'm at her house today taking care of her affairs. Can you come by today?"

"Yeah. I can come today."

I got dressed and asked to borrow Karen's car, telling her that I was going to the lady's house who I'd been calling.

Fifteen minutes later, Kai and I pulled up in front of the house, and we walked up the stairs. *What could her aunt possibly have for me? Maybe it's a book on how to dial or read numbers?* But unfortunately, the door opened before I could knock.

"Sandy?"

"Yes."

"I'm Rose. Please come in."

"Is it okay if my dog comes in?"

"Yes, of course."

Kai and I stepped into a dark foyer, and then Rose led us into a small living room. Heavy red velvet drapes sheltered the room from sunlight. Rose walked over and pulled the drapes back. Beams of light unmasked the life and history of the room and her aunt. "My aunt liked it dark. I think it was her way of knowing her days of traveling were over. She was housebound, but her mind was strong, and she still had her memories." She motioned to an overstuffed dark blue velvet chair, contrasting with the drapes. I sat, with Kai resting at my feet. "Can I get you anything to drink?"

"No, thank you. I'm good."

Rose lowered herself on the couch draped with faded flower sheets. She reached for a picture frame on an antique table dressed with white crocheted doilies. She held the picture in front of me. "This is my Aunt Selma. She was maybe twenty in that photo."

I held the black-and-white picture and looked deep beyond the glass. Selma's light-brown hair had been pulled back slightly, and loose curls fell below her shoulders. My fingers combed through my hair. Because the photo was black-and-white, I couldn't tell what color her eyes were. An angel pendant hung just below her collarbone. *Where did she get that angel necklace? It looks like my guardian angel clip.*

"Selma married late in life and never had children of her own," Rose said.

I stared at the angel.

"Both her and my uncle traveled quite a bit. I wouldn't be surprised if they didn't visit every country."

I handed the picture back.

"A few days ago, I came to visit, and she told me about your phone messages. It was hard for her to get to the phone, so she let the calls go to the answering machine most of the time. She would play the messages back when she could. She listened to them over and over. Your travels brought back memories of when she was young and how she loved exploring new places and meeting new people. She would tell me over and over that the people you meet and the beauty of the kindness of strangers are all a part of your journey, wherever your journey takes you. When she told me about your calls and your travels, her face would light up, and her eyes sparkled." Rose held her hand over her chest. "Then she would tell me her own stories, remembering every detail like it happened yesterday. Which leads me to what my aunt wanted to give you if you called again." She walked to the dining room table cluttered with boxes and packing paper, then walked back to me. In her hands was a deep purple geode, sparkling in the flicker of sunlight beaming through the open drapes. My eyes lit up. "Selma loved hearing about your travels and especially about you trying to find a geode of your own. There's one story my aunt often told me about when she and my uncle were in Uruguay. After days of hiking and exploring, they found a rock they thought could be a geode. They were both so excited. They hurried back to town and found a gemologist and had it cracked open. After months of searching in several countries, she said finding that rock, the anticipation of carrying it back to town and waiting and carefully watching them cut it open, nearly killed her. Would it be beautiful inside, or would it be just another rock?"

I sat on the edge of the chair, listening to her tell the story, my eyes fixed on the geode. "And as you can see, it's a geode, and it's beautiful. She cherished this geode. It was something that I don't even think *she* knew what she was looking for, but when Aunt Selma found it, she knew that what was inside was what she'd been searching for." Rose held her arms out to me. "She wanted you to have this."

Kai lifted his head when I took the geode from her hands. It was so beautiful and heavy. This geode had a history—Selma's history, and now it would be my story. After searching for a geode for several weeks, I finally had one. My eyes misted with tears. I had to blink several times to hold them back. I cleared my throat quietly. "Are you sure?"

Rose smiled. "Yes, I'm very sure. Selma wanted you to have this." Rose walked back to her chair and sat down. "My aunt wanted you to know that something so plain and rough on the outside can be beautiful on the inside. You just have to be willing to crack the hard shell around it." Rose pulled a piece of paper from her pocket and unfolded it. "My aunt found this poem in a magazine, and she would quote this to all her nieces." She read it out loud.

> "Give a girl wings, and she'll fly around the world.
>
> Tell her a story so she'll know how to dream.
>
> Tell her she is loved so one day she'll know how to love.
>
> Tell her she is beautiful so she'll see the beauty in others.

Rose handed it to me. "You should keep this too."

My head nodded. My heart was heavy. "Thank you. It's so beautiful." Kai rested his head on my knee next to my geode. "That's such a pretty angel necklace your aunt had on in the picture. Do you know where she got it?"

Rose tilted her head to the side. "Angel necklace?" She picked up the picture. "I don't see a necklace in this picture." Rose handed the photo to me.

There was no necklace. *I swear there was an angel pendant around her neck. What happened to it?* "Oh, ah, I must have been seeing things." I stood. "I think I should get going. Ah, Kai needs to go home now." Kai and Rose followed me to the door. "Thank you so much for the geode. I'll never forget this day or your Aunt Selma. I'm sorry I didn't get to meet her."

"You are most welcome. And thank you for your phone messages to my aunt even though they were by accident." Rose beamed. "Sometimes accidents are meant to happen."

TWENTY-ONE

I Learned to Walk While You Were Away

I sat the geode in the back seat and jumped in the front. Kai climbed up in the front passenger seat. "Kai, you saw the angel necklace, right?"

Kai panted and licked the window. I lowered the window to get some fresh air. "Kai, there was a necklace around Selma's neck. I know I saw it." Kai ignored me. *Maybe I didn't see it. Maybe I wanted to see it.* I tugged Kai's ear. "Kai, what do you think she meant when she said she wanted me to know that something so plain and rough on the outside can be beautiful on the inside, but you have to be willing to crack the hard shell around it? Do you think she was talking about me? Am I that hard on the outside? Is this why my mother left me? And why JD broke up with me? Or is this what I've become because of my mother? Will I grow old like Selma and never have children? It's not that I don't want to try. That's not what scares me." I thought for a minute. "I'm afraid of crashing. Maybe nobody will ever love me." I leaned my head back against the headrest and closed my eyes. "Maybe I am a plain old rock." My eyes opened. "Kai, you're not helping me." Kai sat up and licked my face, then turned

213

and looked out the window. "You love me, though." *I don't need anyone else.*

When we got home, I took the geode inside. Karen and Kelsey were in the kitchen. Kai ran over to Kelsey, wagging his tail. "It looks like Kai's leg is a lot better," Karen said.

"Yeah, it looks that way."

"Well, how did it go?" Karen asked.

I placed the geode on the table. "I had been looking for a geode the whole time we were traveling. But I didn't find one. Except in the gift shop at Monument Valley, but I couldn't afford one." I told Karen the rest of the story about Selma and her search for geodes.

"That was nice of Selma and Rose."

"I know it was. Do you want to hear something really strange?"

"You called someone else by mistake again?" Karen giggled.

My eyes narrowed. "No. When Rose showed me a picture of Selma, I thought I saw an angel pendant around her neck. But when Rose looked at it and then handed the photo to me again, there wasn't one. Isn't that weird?"

Karen studied my face. "Sometimes we see what we want to believe is there."

What's that supposed to mean?

"Don't forget to register for school."

"I won't, but I have to go. I forgot to get gas in your car before I came home. I'll be right back."

I pulled up to the pump at the gas station where Holly and I filled up before leaving on our trip. "Kai, this is where it all began. I met a gray-haired man that told me about geodes. He acted as if he knew me, somehow. After we talked, all I wanted was to find a geode, to see what was so special inside,

214

but I didn't find any geodes." I held Kai's sweet face in my hands. "I found you instead." After I filled the car and paid for the gas, I opened the passenger door. Kai jumped down. "Let's go inside. I want you to meet him."

The door chimed when we walked in. A man with red hair who looked to be in his thirties was behind the counter. "Can I help you?"

"Ah, yeah. About a month ago, I was in here, and an older man was working. He had long gray hair. Is he here?"

The man squinted his eyes and shook his head. "No, there isn't anyone who matches that description working here."

Kai barked three times and nudged my leg. I pulled him close to me. "Are you sure? Maybe he quit or something?"

"I'm sure. I own this place, and nobody like that has worked here." Kai pawed at my leg again. I watched him walk over to the wood rack with brochures near the door and sit down. I scanned the brochures and found one just like the one the old man had given me. I held the brochure up. "He gave me this."

"I don't know what to tell you. Nobody like that has worked here. Maybe it was another gas station?"

"No. I'm sure this was the place." Kai barked. I looked down at him. "I guess we should go, Kai."

As we drove away, I looked over at Kai. "What is going on?" Kai tilted his head. "I know I saw that man. And...and that angel necklace around Selma's neck." Kai turned and stared out the side window. "Am I crazy, Kai?" *Or do I see what I want to believe?*

Before dinner, I registered over the phone for beauty school in Denver. Classes were starting in six weeks. I'm glad I did because they only had one daytime opening left, and Karen and I still had to go find an apartment and a job.

Kai and I took a long walk to the Tastee Freeze downtown after dinner. I tied Kai up to the bike rack and walked to the door. Kai pulled on the leash and barked. My heart shuddered. I walked back to him and rubbed his head. "Kai, you're going to be okay. I'm not leaving you. I'll bring you back a treat. It's okay." Kai barked and pulled on the leash again. "Screw it. You can come in with me." I unhooked him, and we walked inside. "No barking, now, or they'll throw us out," I whispered. Kai looked around and then sat next to me in line. A few children dressed in uniforms were rambunctious and loud ordering their ice cream. After the girls ordered and paid, I ordered a root beer float and a small vanilla cone for Kai. We stepped aside and waited for our order. The children took their cones and chattered on the way out the door. Kai and I watched them leave. Finally, the counter girl called our order, and I reached for Kai's cone and my float.

A familiar voice said, "Hi, Sandy."

I turned. "JD." He stood in front of me with a large root beer float. "How have you been?"

I tried to balance Kai's leash and Kai's ice cream cone while he jumped up to reach it.

"Let me help you." JD took Kai's cone. Kai turned and danced in front of JD.

"Ah, I'm good." I licked my lips. *Damn it. I forgot to put on lip gloss.* When JD wasn't looking, I pinched my lips to force a little color into them. "I think we should go outside before he makes a mess." Kai led the way out. As we sat at a table, I couldn't help but notice how JD looked exceptionally nice in khaki shorts and a short-sleeve shirt. My heart drummed in my chest. *I thought I forgot about him.*

"Who's the cone for?"

"Oh, it's for Kai."

JD handed it to me. "Are you a dog walker now?"

"What? Ah, no. Kai is my dog." I lowered the cone. Kai licked twice then covered the cone with his mouth. I pulled the cone away. "Kai, you can't eat the whole thing. Take small bites." Kai bit the top part off and chewed it. Small pieces of the sugar cone crumbled to the ground.

"I don't think Kai wants to take small bites." JD laughed.

"I guess not." I held the cone for Kai and glanced at JD and then quickly looked away when Kai jumped and snatched the rest of the cone out of my hand.

"How long have you had Kai?"

"I found him on our way home from our trip out West."

"Nice. Who did you go with?"

"Holly, my friend from Chicago." I swirled the straw and took a few sips of my float. "So, what have you been doing since graduation?"

JD started talking, but I was only half-listening. *Can JD see how much I wanted him to kiss me? I want a sexy, hot, spicy kiss. Just like the first kiss we had leaning into his Jeep around midnight last October. I wanted to be his that night, but he belonged to Jessica. But it didn't stop me from kissing him. God, I want his lips on mine.* I closed my eyes for a second, imagining that kiss but better. JD pushing his tongue inside to meet mine. Inch by inch, our bodies grew closer, my heart pounding. A wet tongue swiped across my face. My eyes opened. "Kai!"

JD laughed." I think that's a thank you kiss for the ice cream."

I wiped my face. "Go sit over there, Kai," I said, pointing to the wall next to me.

"I think Kai had the right idea."

"What do you mean?"

JD's cheeks reddened, and his eyes followed mine until they met. "I'd like to kiss you too."

Did he really say that, or did I just imagine that too?

"Very funny, JD. But that was a very impulsive thing to say…."

A teasing smile flashed on his face, then disappeared. "I'm sorry…but…."

"Um, when are you leaving for college? CU Boulder, right?"

"I just told you."

"I'm sorry. I wasn't listening." *I was too busy daydreaming.*

"I leave in two weeks."

"Me too, well, in six weeks."

"Where are you going?"

"Denver. Beauty School."

JD lifted his head. "Oh yeah. I remember you talked about that in school when Jason teased you about being a beauty school dropout, like, um, what was her name in *Grease?*

I rolled my eyes. "Frenchy."

"Ah, yeah. I'm sorry," JD said.

"Except I'm not going to be like Frenchy." *I'm going to finish school, and I'm going to be somebody.*

"I know, you'll be great, whatever you do." There was a moment of silence. "Sandy, I still feel bad for the way we broke up. I was so stupid to do that to you…I…um, maybe we could hang out before we both leave for school. Kinda like…."

Kai jumped up and barked.

I pulled him near me. "What's wrong, buddy?"

Kai continued to bark. I got up and grabbed Kai's leash. "I think I should be going."

"All right. I'll walk you to your car," JD said.

"I walked."

"Okay, then I'll give you a ride home."

Kai circled me, wrapping his leash around my legs. "What are you doing, Kai? You're acting so weird."

JD pointed. "My Jeep is right over there."

Kai looked up at me and shook his head. *Just because he's good looking, doesn't mean he's good for you. Just because he's good looking, doesn't mean he's good for you. Back away, don't be stupid.* I rolled my shoulders back and untangled my legs from Kai's leash. "I think Kai and I are going to walk home."

"All right. Call me if you want to do something before I leave."

Kai jumped in front of me and barked.

JD raised his hands. "Settle down, buddy. I don't think your dog likes me."

"That's so strange. He's never done anything like this," I said, pulling Kai away. "Ah, if I don't see you before you leave, enjoy college life."

"Yeah, you too, Sandy."

I will.

JD jumped in his Jeep. I watched him drive away and waved goodbye. "Kai, did I do the right thing?" Kai licked my hand and nudged my leg and then was silent the rest of the way home. *I forgot about you once. I'll forget about you again.*

219

Six weeks later, a row of moving boxes were open on my bedroom floor. I filled them with clothes and shoes from my closet and dresser drawers. From the top drawer, I pulled out photos of JD and myself. One where JD took me snow skiing. I was dressed as if I knew how to ski in the picture, but I didn't know how. I tried and failed, but at least I tried. I smiled and then broke into a laugh. The next picture was of JD and me at homecoming, and we were so darn cute together. I glanced up at the mirror above my dresser. I'm not cute anymore. I'm not the same girl I was in that image. But I'm… I'm ready. I tossed the picture in the box and taped it up.

I glanced around the empty room, then closed the door and left without turning back.

Kelsey, Kai, and I rode in the back seat. Karen and Dan were in the front. I watched the mountains shrink in the landscape as we drove closer to the city. When we pulled up to the apartment where I was going to be sharing with another girl, I gazed out in the distance. The mountains of Breckenridge were still there, only smaller, but they were still there. I may have left, but they hadn't left me.

Dan and Karen helped me move my boxes into my new room. Kelsey held Kai's leash.

Dan placed the last box on the floor. "Well, that's it, the last box."

"Don't forget your orientation is at three o'clock this afternoon," Karen said.

"Yep. I got the schedule."

"And you have your bus pass?"

I reached in my back pocket and pulled it out. "Yep, right here."

"Okay, let's get going," Dan said.

I followed Dan, Karen, and Kelsey out to the car. I wrapped Kai's leash around my hand several times. I didn't want to let go.

Karen held her arms out. "This is goodbye." She hugged me tightly. "Be safe. Study hard. And I hope you know you will always have a place to come back to. Oh, and you have my number, right?"

"Ha-ha. Yes, Karen, I have your number. Thanks for everything Karen."

Dan walked over and hugged me. "Never stop being yourself. And if you get bored, you can always follow the White Rabbit."

"The White Rabbit?"

"Dan," Karen yelled. "Don't tell her that."

"*Alice in Wonderland*," Dan said.

"Oh, Yeah, got it."

I looked over at Kelsey standing by the car door. When our eyes met, she hung her head in tears. "Kelsey, aren't you going to say goodbye to me?"

She shook her head.

"Why not?"

"Because I don't want you to leave."

"I'm coming back. And besides, you get to keep Kai for me and take care of him."

She nodded and slowly smiled. "I'll take good care of Kai."

I bent down and hugged her. "I know you will."

"Kai, it's your turn." I walked a few steps away with Kai while Dan, Karen, and Kelsey got in the car. I knelt, "Kai, Karen, and Dan are good people. They're going to take good care of you. They saved me and took me in when my mother left me. Kind of like I saved you when your douchebag owner abandoned you. So, you will never have to worry about being

221

tied to a fence again and left behind ever again." I held his face to mine. "Thank you." Tears filled my eyes. They rolled down my face. "Thank you for saving me too, by giving me something to love all my own," I whispered in his ear. "I'll never forget you." Kai swiped his tongue over my face. "I like how you know when I need a kiss."

I walked Kai to the car. Kelsey held the back door open for him, and he jumped in and then looked back at me. We both smiled. He settled in next to Kelsey, and she closed the door.

At ten minutes to three, I walked into the beauty school. I took a seat down front. Promptly at three o'clock, a long gray-haired man and a woman stood in front. "Welcome," the woman said. She was wearing an angel pendant necklace.

Sometimes you hang on and sometimes you let go—I'm ready to let go and be a Cactus Girl forever.

She spread her wings and forged her own path.

THE END

In a world where you can be anything
be a Cactus Girl.